Love on Moonlight Lake

Adriana Sargent

Copyright © 2024 by Adriana Sargent

All rights reserved.

No part of this publication may be reproduced, distributed, or transmitted in any form or by any means, including photocopying, recording, or other electronic or mechanical methods, without the prior written permission of the publisher, except as permitted by U.S. copyright law. Email authoradrianasargent@gmail.com with any questions.

The story, all names, characters, and incidents portrayed in this production are fictitious. No identification with actual persons (living or deceased), places, buildings, and products is intended or should be inferred.

Book Cover by Bretnie

First edition 2024

ISBN 979-8-34449-610-8

*To all the sapphics out there who want a dreamy and steamy holiday romance
they can relate to.
This one is for **us**.*

Chapter One
Gianna

"Tomorrow we should go pick up a tree. I hear that Rufus and Lauren's daughter is still in town. I know you've always had a crush on her."

"*Nan*." I groaned into the phone. She spoke like she didn't know her name, like she hadn't known her since we were in third grade.

"Don't Nan me in that tone, Gianna. You can't fool me; you were always falling over yourself to be near her. Do you remember that time when you chipped your front tooth when you got that skateboard? You were convinced you could..."

I tuned out her voice and glared down at the man before me. He was out of place in his suit and freshly shined shoes. His eyes were wide and the puppy pout on his face made me want to spill oil on his white button-up shirt.

"Maybe that was your plan all along, she did come by the house every day for six weeks to feed you noodles. Don't know why you needed all those noodles for a chipped tooth," Nan continued.

"Thank you for that riveting reminder of my awkward childhood years," I grunted. "I don't know why you act like you haven't fed her the exact same noodles whenever she has a stomachache. We can go, if," I said over her whoop, "you promise not to mention that story to her, or anyone else, ever again."

Nan was silent for a moment, and I knew she was thinking about all the other stories she had. In the last few months, her life mission had been to get me together with my childhood crush. I just wished she chose a different tactic, instead of embarrassing me.

"I promise, darling."

I smiled at her words. "Why do you want to go so early anyway?" I asked, continuing to stare down the man before me. It gave me great joy to see him beg. He looked around the tow truck to the man who was leaning against the door tapping his watch. My smile widened. I wondered if he had to pay extra for keeping the car loaded on the bed.

"I have my reasons," Nan sang. That was never good. Nan's reasons could lean anywhere from an obscure discount that saves her five cents, *every penny matters,* to "accidentally" running into a crush that started in my pubescent years and bled into adulthood.

"That's mighty sketchy, old lady."

Nan hummed as a clanking sound reached me through the speaker. I bet she grabbed a pot and started banging it on the table just to make me think she was busy. She was probably going to one of the mixers her housing complex put together where she didn't need to bring food at all; everything was prepared by specialized cooks. Ever since she moved into the 55 and older community, she partied and told me to mind my business but refuses to mind her own. She loved to mention how I only had something to say about her social life because I didn't have one. Which wasn't true, I had a very healthy social life. Romance was a different story. I hadn't been on a proper date in three years.

"I'll see you tomorrow, Nan. I love you."

"I love you too, darling!" She hung up before I had a chance to lower it from my cheek.

"You shouldn't have bought a manual if you don't know how to drive it, Joe. The transmission is blown," I said, dropping my phone on the counter and crossing my arms.

Joe's mouth gaped in mock horror. "You haven't even looked at it! And I know how to drive a stick, Gianna. This was *not* my fault. I stopped at a stop sign, and she refused to move again!"

I squeezed my fingers tighter on my arms, aware of the grease stains that covered my favorite green flannel.

"Alright, I might have failed to shift a time or two, but I always figured it out in the end... Okay, more than a time or two. What was I supposed to do? You refused to teach me."

"I said I would teach you, Joe. You didn't come back or call me."

"Can you fix it, Gianna? Please. This is my baby."

I rolled my eyes. Joe had a new "baby" every six months, and it only took him two to destroy the beautiful 1970 Superbird. I don't even want to think about what he did to the 1956 Ford he had last year. I still had to fight the urge to punch him. The thought of the hood cracked like an eggshell gave me nightmares.

Of course, I *would* fix his car, even if the thought of putting her in harm's way nearly gave me a conniption. I had been working on Joe's cars since before I opened this shop with my Grandpa, who had been fixing them long before that. The part of me that envied Joe's collection wanted to say no, but I swore I could hear Grandpa telling me I didn't have a choice.

Invisible Grandpa wasn't wrong. Even if we didn't consider how much I loved being the one to bring them back to life after neglect... I needed the money.

There were no skipping jobs when you decided to open a mechanic shop in the middle of nowhere, Colorado. Population of 4,000 did not a successful shop make. Most of these folks took care of their own maintenance, oil changes, and even minor engine repairs. We usually saw the special cases-brake replacements, transmission issues, and complete engine overhauls.

It didn't help that I don't feel right charging the old man who used to babysit me the $2,000 a transmission replacement usually would cost. Not charging those who changed your diapers at some point in your life also proved to be an issue when it came to maintaining a business in a small town.

"I'll see what I can do," I murmured, and Joe's smile was so bright it might have been able to recharge the electricity in the building. "I'm charging you full price, Joseph. Plus interest," I warned with a sigh, taking the keys from him.

"Whatever you need! You're a lifesaver. Don't drop her!" Joe shouted, running out to the tow truck who looked minutes away from cutting the chords.

"You're a softy," Deserea said, standing beside me.

I looked over at her with a snort. "Says the one wearing an elf's hat."

"'Tis the season and all." She eyed my own Santa hat. "Santa does need her helpers." I grinned down at her, flicking the little bell at the tip of her hat. "How's your Nan?" she asked, swatting my hand.

"Obnoxious as ever."

"She still bothering you about that girl?"

I felt my cheeks heat.

That girl.

That.

Girl.

Raven had never been "that girl". She had been my best friend since I was nine years old, and the love of my life since then, too.

"I'm pretty sure I pay you to work, not worry about my business."

"I have to worry about your sex life. You're my boss and your happiness affects mine. But also, your Nan would be the only one asking, and tell me what's more depressing than that?"

I decided not to respond, and Deserea cackled as I walked to the Superbird.

Chapter Two
Raven

"How do you miss a whole three sections, Cheryl?" I asked, staring at the long foliage growing over the cut-your-own-tree section. Cheryl stood beside me with her hand on her hips, looking at the weeds that were trying to bury the beautiful trees, one suffocating vine at a time.

"I can't say, Rav. Must have had one too many hot chocolates," Cheryl said with a shrug and walked towards the mower. "I'll take care of it right now."

"Make sure you clean up when you're done! We still need to get the lights up and we open tomorrow!" I shouted after her.

"Yeah, yeah, don't get your panties in a twist," Cheryl grumbled.

I rolled my eyes and walked over to the drink stand where Stan was straining the apple cider mix. The smell made my heart pull. The recipe was my mother's creation, and her passing was still so fresh in my mind that I had to blink a few times to clear the burning from my eyes.

Though it was a balmy 60 degrees outside a hot cider would take the edge off my nerves. It had been a long time since I was responsible for opening the farm. Sure, I visited plenty and helped as needed, but I was never responsible for opening and running the Tree Farm since I left for college. Preparing for opening day was stressful and took months in the making. Luckily, my parents had taken care of most... A loud purring startled me out of my thoughts and a brown furry body weaved between my legs.

"Hey, Pounce," I said.

The river otter stood on his hind legs and stared up at me, his pale amber eyes burning into mine.

I rolled my eyes and rested my arms on the counter. "Hey, Stan. You wouldn't by chance have any -"

He put a large biodegradable cup on the counter with a smirk and slid a bowl next to it. "Chai tea, milk, sugar, honey, and a large bowl of warm apple cider. Just the way you both like it."

I grinned. "He's your biggest fan, Stan."

"You're damn right he is," he sniffed. But I saw the smile peek from beneath his bushy mustache as he peered over the counter to see the chittering creature.

Pounce gave him a squeak of appreciation and followed me to the porch. He weaved around me in excitement until I put the bowl down and sat in the rocking chair. He wrapped his body around the bowl and started to drink.

I sighed, looking out at the large farm that was preparing the finishing touches for opening day tomorrow. Normally we would open the day after Thanksgiving, but the demand for trees *on* Thanksgiving was too sweet a temptation to deny. So, here we were. I sent a glare Cheryl's way, but she ignored me.

Luckily, enough of us at the farm didn't celebrate Thanksgiving because of religious or cultural beliefs, so no one was working when they would otherwise be spending time with their family. It also helped that they were getting paid extra.

Rachel tipped her head at me as she escorted a few goats across to the petting zoo area. The tractor was being cleaned and the trailer for guests was being attached to it. The sleigh was being touched up and the horses brushed. For the most part, the farm was a well-oiled machine; the seasonal workers were well-versed in the requirements of the farm. Every year was special, but this one was different. Even the decorations were inspiring. As if they were trying to outdo everything they had ever done in the past, as if this was a celebration for more.

"This is going to be a busy year," I murmured to Pounce.

He purred.

"Maybe we can go back to Rocky Mountain after this, or maybe Montana, or even Arizona. I've never been there," I said into my cup. Being a Park Ranger had its perks and the ability to move around was the biggest one.

Pounce stopped drinking to look at me and let out a sound that told me he was not impressed. I chuckled. Even if I did plan to leave, my father was in no state for me to go anytime soon. When Pounce finished his cider, he found a patch of sun on the porch, flopping onto his back and abruptly passing out. I rolled my eyes.

Lazy.

"Must be nice to enjoy a break, boss!" Cheryl shouted as she finally shut off the mower.

I rolled my eyes again. "If you didn't miss an entire row, you could be on a break as well!" I shouted back. "And put up that mower before you even think about a hot toddy," I warned.

She laughed, waving over one of the other workers to put up the mower. I tried to hide a smile as she walked over to Stan, who had a cup of spiked cider already waiting. I watched as she leaned over the counter and kissed him.

My heart lurched at that show of affection.

"Nope!" I grunted, standing up and walking towards the stairs. "We are not going to do that!" I looked to Pounce to see if he might follow me, but he was basking in the sunlight, his amber eyes watching me in a way that said, "If you try to move me, I will maim you".

"I didn't want your company anyway," I said to him. He purred and closed his eyes. I grabbed his bowl, putting it on the table next to the door to remind myself to wash it. I stomped down the stairs and smiled at the squeak of irritation from the river otter before grabbing a handful of boxes containing lights and heading over to the freshly mowed rows that needed to be just as festive as the rest.

It was a long day's work, but in the end, we all stood back and admired our efforts. With the sun just setting, the solar-powered lights gradually illuminated. The lights from the Welcome Center dimmed and then... there was snow. A dusting settled over us and the trees. Pounce squeaked in excitement and started spinning in circles in the large opening before us. Stan served us all a cup of warm cider and we just watched as darkness overtook the tree farm. All that was missing was my dad... and my mom.

I can do this.

Chapter Three
Gianna

"We got another one," Ryan said before he dropped an envelope onto the keyboard in front of me. Big red letters of **Third Notice** stamped across the top.

"Lovely. Thanks, Ryan," I murmured as I placed the envelope to the side. I didn't bother opening it, I already knew what it said.

It's not like we were far behind on rent, just a few months. Which was unfortunately, a couple hundred away from ten thousand. I shuffled my feet, my boots feeling uncomfortably tight. The sounds of the shop made the ring in my ears grow louder. Normally, it was a good sound, it meant we have business, but it wasn't enough business to keep us afloat. I opened a browser, entered the loan website, and paid one month with sweaty hands. Luckily, I knew one of the loan officers from the bank and he gave me a few pointers on how to keep the shop from getting closed, as well as how to make the payments in a way that won't flag the company. At least until I could come up with the money to get back on track.

I logged off the computer and fished for the keys from the drawer before grabbing my helmet. I had to get the hell out of here.

"I'll be back," I called to Deserea.

She slid out from beneath a car with a raised brow and a nod. "Got it, boss. Don't forget Mr. Marshall is dropping the car off around four and you know he won't let anyone but you touch it."

I glanced at the time. "I'll be back at three."

It was perfect weather for a ride. Even though it was the day before Thanksgiving, the sun was bright and the weather cool. One of the best things about Colorado was having a snowless spring day in the middle of winter. The chrome and silver of my bike had been shined and it sparkled in the light like an invitation. I straddled the warm leather seat and kicked it on. My body relaxed almost immediately when it rumbled to life. The sound of the bike blocked out all other thoughts as I snapped my helmet closed. The Bluetooth clicked on, and I let the music settle into my bones as I pulled out of the parking lot.

It had been weeks since I last took a long drive. I only started riding when one of my clients from the shop told me about his 1990 Harley Davidson Fat Boy that he had been unable to ride because of an injury. After some finagling, I purchased Fatty from him two years ago and I'd been riding any, and every, chance I got. The mountains of Colorado provided such beautiful scenery that I took Fatty more than I took my truck. Only a few thousand were ever made and what it cost me justified how much I rode, making it also one of the best ways to get out of my head.

I turned off the main road and hit the highway, letting the vibration of the bike and the music pull me away. The road and cars I passed turned into a colorful blur as I picked up speed. The sky was nearly cloudless, and the sun beat down on my arms as I veered around a car and shifted into the next gear.

It was always Grandpa's dream to open a mechanic shop. He taught me everything I knew about working on cars, and for that, I owed him everything. I opened this shop for him and for that little nine-year-old girl who was so angry at the loss of her parents. Grandpa was the one who taught me to channel my anger into something constructive. We built dozens of engines from junk yards, helped repair countless cars, and all the while, blaring bluegrass, rock n' roll, and whatever else was needed, depending on the day I had.

Grandpa left me a small inheritance and I used it to open the shop. The thought of failure meant that I failed him. I could not live with myself knowing that I had not done everything I could. Nan was the light that we both needed after a long day's work in the garage. However, she never took the excuse of being greasy or oily as a reason to not help with cooking or cleaning.

There were thousands of things I could thank my grandparents for. The most important one was taking me in when my parents died and showing me the value of hard work and persistence.

However, none of those attributes were helpful with a failing business. I liked to think of myself as the hardest working person in Caswell, Colorado, but that meant nothing if I didn't have the customer base.

I shifted into fifth gear and let Fatty take me where he wanted.

"Happy Thanksgiving, Nan," I said, kissing her cheek. "Who are all of these people and what are they drinking?" There were over a dozen elderly people with red solo cups standing around her cramped apartment. She grabbed my arm, since my hands were full of food, and pulled me into the space where the bodies immediately made me overheat.

"Mimosas, darling!" Nan shouted, and I noticed a red cup in her hand as well. "This is only my second cup, but Charlene is the bartender and I'm convinced she forgets to pour the orange juice!"

"I waft the juice, Margie. We don't want to overpower the Brut!" Charlene responded while standing next to six bottles of champagne; I recognized her from my many visits to Nan's. There was a bottle of juice as well, but it looked completely untouched which confirmed Nan's suspicions. I set the food on the counter, watching as she lifted her hand over the opening of the orange juice and fanned whatever nonsensical substance over the full-to-the-brim cup of champagne.

She smiled, grabbed the cup, and handed it to me. "Happy Thanksgiving!"

"Uh…" I looked over at Nan to see her smacking someone's hand who reached for the macaroni and cheese I brought. "Thank you." I took the cup and tried to steady it as Charlene clanked her full cup against it. It's not that I had never met these people before, but in the few years that Nan had lived here, it seemed that her parties grew by a few dozen people each time.

"Drink up, Gi," Nan said, in a stage whisper. "Laurel made the cornbread and it's drier than The Atacama."

"I heard that, you old trout. My cornbread is the talk of Mount Pleasant. I still get calls from friends about how much they miss it," Laurel said, waving her cane around, almost whacking someone to her right.

The black lady who almost got taken out, I recognized as Rachel, grabbed the cane, and smacked Laurel's butt with it. "You know they only call you to make sure you're never coming anywhere near South Carolina again with that dry-ass cornbread." Laurel wrapped her arm around Rachel as they laughed together.

"Don't forget, Nan, we have to go get your tree this evening," I murmured, trying to bite back a smile.

Nan waved me off. "I am old enough to know how to control my alcohol. Tom! Come over here and help Gianna cut the turkey. I swear, I invite these old grumps to my house, and they forget their manners."

"Margie, love, you never let anyone in this kitchen on a regular day let alone a holiday. How was I supposed to know you were ready for me?" Tom said, his cane bearing most of his weight. I grabbed the turkey from the oven and pulled back the foil.

"You know I'm always ready for you, Tom," Nan purred.

"I'm going to be sick," I grumbled and downed the rest of my orange-scented champagne. Whoever said partying with the elderly was wholesome obviously never met my Nan's friends.

Chapter Four
Raven

One of the things I missed most about my old job was the freedom.

Being a park ranger wasn't easy, not in the slightest. Knowing that you were responsible for dozens, if not hundreds, of lives was terrifying. If that phone call came in, you would have to respond and potentially save a life or lives. If that person died, you would be the one drilled with questions: what happened, your location, was the area secured and more.

As terrifying as it was, it was also invigorating. It was a great way to channel my need for control, adventures, and discipline. One of my favorite things to do was take groups on hiking trails. Some of the groups loved to challenge me with the hardest hikes, even wanting to repel cliffs (I would never). Others liked seeing nature as it was. I enjoyed taking them to my favorite trails. Ones that were off the beaten path where, if they were quiet enough, they could see a side of nature that existed before we started destroying forests. It was on one of those hikes where I found Pounce.

The sweet river otter's mother had been killed for her babies. Pounce had somehow escaped their grasp but was left barely alive near a river bend between some bushes. We always kept emergency medical kits on hand, and luckily, the group I was with was more concerned about getting the otter to safety than continuing on their hike. They helped me bring him back to the Welcome Center, and a few months later, the hikers received photos in the mail of a healthy Pounce.

He had formed an attachment to me, and since I had minored in Wildlife Rehabilitation in college, I was able to keep him. Not that he belonged to me. In reality, he adopted me. And until he decided he was done with me and wanted sanctuary, we would be together. When I first took him to a rehabilitation center, he would scream and fight until I was back with him, then he would fall asleep. He would look for me until I came to visit and check on his progress, and then he would burrow in my lap, clawing at me with loud squeaking sounds-indignant at my audacity to leave.

The center realized that he would pretend to be sick so I would come to check on him, and once I was there, he was miraculously better. We eventually caught onto his game, but really, we were more impressed at his intellect. It was easy to give him what he wanted, or that's what I convinced the center. I doubt they believed ,me but after his antics continued for almost a year, he was allowed to come home with me. He loved being out in the wild, running around the forests, playing in whatever body of water was nearby, and terrorizing the squirrels.

That was until a few months ago when I had to come back to my childhood home-where I had to be for the farm's first opening since mom died. When I first suggested opening today, I was surprised at how many people were willing to work. Although Colorado law does not say we have to pay time and a half for working on a holiday, I planned to give a little holiday bonus to those who did.

We had a few hours before we opened so we were working hard on the final preparations. Stan whistled at his drink stand and winked at me as he secured the pinecone garland to the opening of the stand before he started setting out napkins. Cheryl arranged the boxes of ornaments and markers for people to claim their trees with. The netting for the trees was organized and the animals were cared for by the farm hands.

I couldn't help my smile as I turned and ascended the short staircase to the shop, Pounce right on my heels. It felt less hectic in the store as Yari was the only one there. Her bright pink micro braids were topped with a black hat that said "Yule This" in white block letters.

"Hey boss, hey Pounce!" she said with a bright smile.

"Yari," I warned.

"I know, I know. It's just so funny calling you that, you always get so grumpy."

I rolled my eyes. Pounce walked behind the counter to the little bed laid for him beneath the cash register and let out a large huff as he settled into the warmth. "Why do you get so grumpy by the way? Haven't you always been a boss? At the very least, you've always been a boss ass bitch. I looked it up and like only 30 percent of park rangers are women. Can you believe that? You are one of 30 percent. That's amazing. I could never do that. What would happen if you came up to a bear? I've read that you're supposed to play dead, but what happens if they decide to check that you're actually dead and you get bitch slapped by a bear! Would it be called bear slapped? I bet it feels like getting hit by a truck?"

My mom hired Yari as the store manager two years ago, she was in her second year of college, and she had not stopped talking since. I think that's why my mom loved her; she hated the quiet and that's one thing Yari had never been. I didn't interrupt or ask her to stop as we put the finishing touches on the gift shop.

"That's a great choice, ma'am. The Norway Spruce is one of my favorites," I said smiling at the child, her face flushed with excitement. "Are you planning to head over to the petting zoo?" I asked her father. I could see his own childish excitement reflected on his face.

The way the little girl's mouth dropped open, I feared I either wrapped him in something he didn't want to do or ruined a surprise.

"A petting zoo!" the little girl squealed. "Can we go, Dad? Please can we go?" I grimaced and mouthed "sorry" to him.

He waved the apology off and bent to her level. His hands on his knees and face playfully thoughtful. "I don't know, Clara. Do you think they might want special Clarcuddles?"

Clara nodded; her blue eyes bright.

"Okay, put the ornament on the tree and let's go."

Clara took the pink ornament from him with the name "George and Clara Thistle" and dropped it onto the highest branch she could reach, at my hip, and grabbed his hand, dragging him down the tree aisle.

"I'll have this wrapped and ready by the time you're done!" I shouted after them, shoving the order sheet into the dad's hands.

"Merry Christmas!" he said as they rounded the corner towards the hayrides, the opposite direction of the zoo.

I opened my mouth to say something but decided against it. They would have ended up at the hayride anyway... probably.

I sighed and looked back at the seven-foot tree that they picked out. My gloved hands perched on my hips as I stared up at it, squinting into the sunlight. I guess it's lucky that I don't have to cut it down myself. I turned and walked back through the aisle towards the center of the farm.

"Greg!" I called, smiling at some patrons as I passed. "Please let me know if you need some help," I said to the family, cheerily. "Greg!" I shouted louder this time as I approached the gift shop. "Greg!" The jerk was probably elbow deep in caramel popcorn. "Greg, we have a seven-footer that if I try to move, I will be crushed like a music box ballerina figurine, please help!"

"Calm down you little hellion, you're scaring the children," Greg grunted, standing from the rocking chair beside me.

I yelped with a jump. I hadn't even seen him there. Hand on my chest, I pointed behind me. "Norway Spruce, lane 32. Big pink ornament and the children are fine." I glanced over to one who couldn't have been more than four and was staring at me with her mouth wide open. I mimed closing my mouth, and she snapped hers shut.

Welcome to Moonlight Lake Tree Farm where we have a 34-year-old crazy woman screaming about a music box ballerina.

On the plus side, it was the best turnout had, had on opening day in a very long time. At least that's what the numbers said. People decorated their houses earlier and earlier every year. They were desperate to bring joy in before they would have in the past. Pounce was also an animal that most children would never see domesticated. He loved attention and the otter zoomies told me he reveled in being at the very center of it.

"Well, well, well. Look at this beauty." I froze, a wide grin spreading across my face. The four-year-old's eyes widened with alarm, and she tugged her mom's pants. I would recognize that voice anywhere.

"Nan Margie," I squealed and hurled myself into her arms. "I wasn't expecting you until this weekend!" Her small limbs wrapped around me, and she patted my head in a way that made my heart squeeze. I caught a faint whiff of champagne and held back a laugh. Nan was several inches shorter than me, but I had always felt so small and loved in her embrace. After all the years of having her in my life, no one ever hugged me better. I swallowed back a lump in my throat as her arms squeezed me in a way, I didn't know I needed. I used to talk to Nan every day, but after the funeral, I used the excuse of preparing the farm to not contact anyone. I couldn't handle the pity, but I should have known better when it came to Nan Margie.

"I know, baby," Nan whispered kissing my cheek. "Gianna here just couldn't wait another day to see you."

A gasp from beside us made me pull away. I subconsciously smoothed down my hair and shirt before realizing I had ridiculous cartoon tree gloves on. I hastily pulled them off and turned to the person beside Margie.

Somehow, I had missed the 5'11" woman that haunted my dreams since I was nine. I hadn't seen her since my mother's funeral nine months ago. She called incessantly, but I had buried myself deep into the farm and avoided every single call.

Gianna's red hair was freshly cut, the shaved side looked so soft I wanted to nuzzle my face into it. The hair at the top of her head was perfectly styled and a curl fell over her eye. The most amazing eyes I have ever seen. She was born with heterochromia; one of her eyes was blue and the other was brown with a little blue at the top corner. My gaze trailed down past her ridiculously strong jaw, to the peak of skin showing at the neck of her low v-cut shirt that was covered by her flannel, down to her black jeans that hugged her deliciously full thighs.

A cough made my eyes snap up and I met the beautiful ones of Gianna. They sparkled with amusement and her perfect lips quirked up in a smile.

"Hey, Raven," she said, her lips wrapping around my name in a way that made me nearly expire on the spot. "You know you can't trust a word this woman says, she's senile." Gianna looked down at her Nan fondly, and my knees started to shake.

Gianna opened her arms, and I marched like a robot into them. The hug was completely different from Nan's but not any less needed. My head rested against her chest, and the feel of her heartbeat made me want to nuzzle into her. Gianna had been my best friend my entire life, and she always knew what I needed, evident by the space she gave me after I stopped responding to her calls. She didn't take it personally, and she knew I needed the space to figure it out for myself. I never had a moment to think of anything but the farm, Pounce, and sleep. I did send her updates to let her know I was alright, but we hadn't really talked. I realized at that moment how much I missed her.

"Yes, quite. Quite," Nan replied seriously, her eyes sparkling with mischief when we pulled away. "Kind of like that one time when you were fourteen and told dear Raven that the girl, what was her name?"

Gianna looked horrified.

"Tiffany?" I offered, holding back a smile as Gianna's horrified look turned to me.

Nan snapped, "That's the one–Tiffany! I seem to remember you sabotaging that date. Did that happen or is my senile brain confusing me even more?"

I pulled my lips between my teeth trying to hold back a smile. Gianna hated Tiffany the moment she asked me out. The night Tiffany was supposed to pick me up for our date, she never showed. Somehow Gianna knew that I was going to be stood up, brought ice cream and snuck a flask of vodka into the house. We drank, ate ice cream, and talked about how horrible dating was.

"Tiffany stood me up, Nan. She also had a boyfriend and didn't consider dating women to be cheating." I said. I talked to Tiffany later and learned that Gianna had found out that she had a college boyfriend who said she could sleep with any girl she wanted because it wasn't *really* cheating. Having a college boyfriend at 15 was a whole different issue that I tried to reason with her about. She just said I was jealous and immature and never talked to me again.

Nan rolled her eyes. "Some people were just born without good sense. Let me run to the powder room, then I want you to take me to see some trees." I didn't have a chance to respond before the old woman practically ran away, leaving us standing in a sea of bodies as everyone made their way around the farm. She moved rather quickly for a woman pushing 86.

"Glad to see some things haven't changed," I murmured looking up at Gianna. Her eyes were soft, and I knew it went beyond the awkwardness that is Nan Margaret.

"Some have..." she replied, smiling at me. "You look good."

I felt the heat rise to my cheeks and my heart stuttered at her words. A shy smile broke across my face even as I tried to fight it. "So do you," I whispered.

Chapter Five
Gianna

If there was one thing I prided myself on, it was my ability to appear un-bothered by Raven. Which wasn't much of an ability since she was completely oblivious to anyone who had any kind of attraction to her. I was surprised every time she got a new girlfriend. They usually had to be very forward with her, saying they wanted to be with her or they wanted to take her on a date. If anyone said, *"Let's go to dinner"*, she would immediately consider herself friend-zoned. It was always fun to talk through it with her since we called each other after every date. It was the sweetest torture. She knew that she was attractive, she was never shy about that, but when it came to flirting, she was hopeless.

Raven was somehow blind to the fact that I had a crush on her for years, and while hearing about her dates sucked, it was also a great way to find out about the woman in her life.

After the last visit I had with her, I thought she might have had an idea of how I felt but then her mom passed. And even though I chickened out of telling her how I'd felt for over 20 fucking years, the moment was coming to finally admit it.

Neither of us were dating anyone, nor had we been in some time. It never felt like the right time for us. I was also terrified of her rejecting my affections and then I would lose my best friend and be completely humiliated in the same breath.

I had thought for a moment in my 20s that I only had a crush on her because she knew me better than anyone else. However, the feeling never faded. It grew.

"Sorry I haven't been around much," Raven said, her cheeks bright red in shame.

I shook my head. "You know how I was after my parents died. Grieve how you need to; I'm always here for you regardless."

"Better than breaking Brett's nose," she said with a coy smile.

"His nose did not break." I rolled my eyes. "You love to exaggerate that story."

She laughed. "I remember him screaming that you broke it."

"He shouldn't have made fun of me for being an orphan."

"Kids can be cruel."

"Exactly, he never talked about my parents after that now did he?"

Raven snorted. "I don't think he talked much at school *period* after that. Well, until high school. Somehow it became a badge of honor to have had your nose broken at 10."

I still felt no regret for my actions, and the thought of how he turned the other way whenever I was where he tried to walk still brought me joy.

"How's Rufus?" I asked.

I knew that she didn't want to talk about it. If there was one thing I admired most about Raven, it was her strength, but what irritated me was her resistance to having meaningful conversations.

Her dad was stunned after finding out his only child was a lesbian at 13. He had trouble talking to her for a few days after and she refused to talk to me about it as well. *Stubborn ass.*

But after the initial shock, her father became extremely supportive. He bought her first pride flag for her. He did an immense amount of research to ensure he got the right one but couldn't decide which to get her, so he got her every single one and explained to her what they meant.

The last time I visited her, she was in Montana and they were still folded and displayed in her apartment still. It took until then for her to talk to me about what happened.

Even when she said she was Pagan, he was the first to suggest removing "Christmas" from Moonlight Lake Christmas Tree Farm. He tried to call it Moonlight Lake Yule Tree Farm until we were able to convince him that it not only sounded awful, but there was no such thing.

I hadn't seen him since Lauren's funeral either, and from the grimace on Raven's face, he was not doing well.

"He's struggling," she said finally. "He hasn't been down to help much, so I moved back."

I stared at her. I knew she was back to help with the farm, but I assumed she was joking when she said she was moving back. I tried to fight the slight swell of hope that ballooned in my chest.

She's not here for you; calm your horny bits.

Though, the way she practically eye fucked me earlier meant she was still attracted to me. Maybe it was my moment.

"What about your job?" I asked.

"I'll take some shifts in the summer at Rocky Mountain to help with the cost of maintaining the farm and parts of my sanity, but for the most part, I will be here." She shrugged nonchalantly, but her mouth always gave her away. Since we were kids, she had this habit of biting her lips and cheeks to the point of bleeding when she was worried. At that moment, she was chewing the inside of her right cheek.

I knew it was upsetting for her. She loved being a park ranger, and only nine months ago when I visited, she was animated about loving her job. After that trip, I thought everything between us would change. We shared a moment that gave me hope, but when I called her after I landed to tell her how I felt, she told me the news about her mom. Nothing else mattered at that point but getting to her dad's to help however I could. It was a long few weeks, especially when Raven arrived back home.

"How's the shop?" she asked, and I grimaced.

"I don't know why I thought opening a mechanic shop in a small town was a good idea," I answered, rolling my eyes.

"What happened? I thought it was going well."

"It's not that bad yet, but it has been slow for the last few months."

Raven raised a brow. "But you still have Joe and his endless supply of classic cars, right?"

I groaned, shoving a hand through my hair. It flopped back over my brow as I responded, "Every time he brings a new one in, I want to throttle him."

She laughed and I had to keep myself from drooling. She always had the best laugh, the kind that made people stop and stare. Her chocolate eyes sparkled, her head thrown back to expose the long lines of her neck and her tightly curled hair brushing her shoulders.

She was *so* beautiful.

"Now." Nan clapped, approaching. I bet I looked like an idiot standing here staring at Raven. "Let's find me a tree for my boring little apartment. I can't paint the walls so it's always nice to have one of your big trees in the living room. Brightens up the beige walls and adds some joy. You know Tom tried to talk me into putting wallpaper up instead. He offered to help but I saw what he did with his apartment and there is no way I would allow him within 30 feet of adhesive in my house."

"When were you in Tom's apartment, Nan?" I asked, appalled. Grandpa died eight years ago, and I knew she was no saint, but I had no idea she was walking into random men's apartments. Nine times out of 10 when I went to see her, she had either just seen Tom or was seeing him that night.

Nan waved my question away. "That's none of your concern. His walls look like crinkle paper, Raven. What kind of tree do we want this year? Last year I had the Fraser, though, I would have never picked it if Lauren hadn't recommended..." Nan's words trailed off and she winced.

Raven grabbed Nan's hand and wrapped it around her arm, guiding her down an aisle of trees. "She had the best taste, I admit, but I might be able to help find something." Raven held out her other hand and looked at me expectantly. I didn't bother to contain my grin as I offered the woman I had been in love with since I was a child my arm.

I hated to admit the shiver that went through me had nothing to do with the chill in the air, but the feel of her fingers on my bicep. Her grip was tight and I wasn't sure if it was absentmindedly or on purpose, but when she pulled me closer to her and tilted her head on my shoulder as we stepped through the rows of trees, I didn't mind in the slightest.

Chapter Six
Raven

"Dad?" I asked, knocking on the door to his apartment. He hadn't been to the farm since we opened over a week ago and the only communication, we shared were small texts of good morning, good night, and I love you.

Normally, I would count the small blessing of hearing from him, but I feared that he hadn't left the house in over a month. He and mom had shared the cabin on the farm, but once she passed, he moved into an apartment and I moved into the cabin. He said he heard her laughter in every space, and he couldn't stand the idea of staying there anymore, even if he switched rooms.

The cabin on the farm was a decent size with two bedrooms and two and a half bathrooms, but it wasn't large enough to erase the memories. Even though we found him a good apartment, it wasn't somewhere he should hibernate. He needed to get out, to breathe in some fresh air.

I jiggled the key into the lock and opened the door. "Dad?" I called again as I peeked inside. Relief coursed down my back when I noticed how clean it was. I was concerned that he had dug into a hole of depression like I did. It took Gianna calling me back-to-back (even if I didn't answer) and sending local friends in Montana to my place for me to get out of bed. After that, it was days of cleaning and therapy to get back to a semblance of my life. That was before I moved back home.

"In here, sweetie!" his baritone voice came from the bedroom. "Can you bring the hammer? It's in the top drawer in the kitchen, between the fridge and microwave. Above the cutlery and on top of the painting you drew for me when you were five. I remember that day like yesterday, you were so proud of yourself." His chuckle sent a wave of relaxation through my body. He continued to talk as I grabbed the hammer and walked into his room.

"It was your first day of kindergarten. Do you remember? I didn't realize they would have you bring home artwork. Your mother had to elbow me in the ribs because I tried so hard not to laugh when you told me what it was supposed to be. Do you remember what it was?"

I bit my lip smiling as I grabbed the picture and unfolded it, flattening it on the kitchen counter. I laughed at the image my five-year-old self had created. It was a family portrait, but I added a blob that was supposed to be a cat in my arms. It was my attempt at getting a pet... It didn't work.

"Did you get the hammer?" Dad yelled.

I rolled my eyes, but my smile did not falter I folded the drawing, grabbed the tool from the drawer, and stowed the drawing away. When I stepped into the bedroom, I was accosted by the most repulsive wallpaper I had ever seen. It was a hodgepodge of flowers and bugs in red, green, and yellow.

"What the hell is that, Dad?" I asked. He waved me over to where he stood holding a nail in the wall that the monstrosity covered.

"What? You don't like it? I've always wanted something like this. Your mother hated bugs, so I thought no time like the present."

I handed him the hammer and stood back with my arms crossed as he secured the nail into the wall. His head covered the frame he put up, but when he stepped back and stood beside me, my eyes immediately started burning.

There, in a simple white frame, was the first photo we took at Moonlight Lake Tree Farm. Mom and Dad stood on either side of me, and as sad as I was to leave home, my smile was as bright as their happiness was infectious. The photo was taken by Gianna while her grandparents were right behind her making funny faces, causing outbursts of laughter.

Dad wrapped his arm around my waist. I leaned my head on his shoulder and his dropped to mine as we stared at the photo.

"Good choice," I whispered.

I felt his nod. "I thought so too, kid."

"Are you alright?" I asked quietly. I didn't want to break the peaceful silence, but I came here for a reason. No one had seen him in weeks, and the fact that he was in the apartment whistling and putting up the most awful wallpaper did not assuage my fear. He had shut himself off after mom died, and while I do not fault him for that, it did scare me into thinking I was going to lose both of my parents.

I barely handled mom. Seeing Gianna made me realize how far I pulled into myself. I cut off friends and family, even work, because I was unable to breathe. I cut myself off from the one person who understood me most in the world–Gianna. In doing that, I didn't realize how far my Dad had withdrawn from the world, and by the time I did, it was too late to pull him out of the depths of his depression, especially as I was still circling the drain of my own demise.

When Cheryl called to tell me that he had not been to the farm in weeks and things were falling into disrepair, I used it as the kickstart to leave Montana and move home. If it hadn't been for Pounce and the Tree Farm, I don't know if I would have fully resurfaced. There were still moments where I felt like I was drowning. The pain had been so intense that I would rather feel nothing than the immense weight of loss. Instead, I honed that pain into the Farm and worked to keep it running. When I stepped onto the land all those months ago, it was apparent that everyone had been struggling. My Mom was the light of that place, and without her, it was as if it had lost its soul.

I shoved myself into the work that it took to fix it. To get the foliage cleaned up and nurse the trees back to health. It took months, but everyone helped. It was therapeutic to clean up the neglect, to bring something back to life that was cared for by someone who was gone.

Dad's arm tightened around my waist, and he kissed my head. "I'm doing better. I'm sorry for disappearing on you."

I turned my face into his shoulder to wipe the tears that had spilled. It made me feel like a teenager again, when I would cry on his shoulder until he was soaked. He told me he cherished the moments that I was vulnerable with him.

"I don't blame you, Dad," I whispered.

"Oh, kid," he said. He turned fully towards me and wrapped his arms around me as I cried. Even at 34 years old, the feeling of crying in my Dad's arms was comforting. He soothed circles on my back and rocked us side to side as he allowed me to cry months' worth of pent-up tears on his red flannel.

I don't know how long I cried. Simply that he stood there with me, whispering that it was alright. My eyes hurt by the time I finished, and when I turned my head to the side, the room had descended into darkness as the sun started to set.

"That wallpaper is really awful," I said.

He laughed, the sound making me smile.

"Yeah, it is. I love it though," he said.

"Me too."

Chapter Seven
Gianna

"Sorry, Sir. We are fully booked today, but if you can leave the vehicle overnight, we can work on it first thing in the morning." My heart was pounding in my ear so loud that I almost missed the response from the guy over the phone.

"I'll bring it by in a few hours," he said.

My smile didn't falter as I hung up the phone and made a note about the Mustang that needed an oil change, tire rotation, balance, and potentially new brakes. I didn't know what happened, but in the last week, business had picked up exponentially. I was able to pay the rest of September's rent which meant we were only three months behind. I even placed a large order for some tools that needed to be replaced, including a new engine lift.

"If you're done standing over there grinning, I could use your help." Deserea's voice was nearly a growl.

I raised a brow and looked over at her. She pointed to a vehicle that was parked on a lift, ready to go up as she stood beneath another and was working the drain plug. I glanced down at my watch.

"I can do one right now, then I'm meeting Raven for lunch," I said as I walked over. I heard the pop of the plug and oil started to pour into the catch pan.

Deserea's head snapped over to me with a wide grin on her full cheeks.

"Don't you start." I warned.

"I would never!" she answered a little too gleefully. "Just glad to see she took pity on you enough to talk to you again. It was difficult to watch the brooding. It was a little pathetic actually."

Jack grunted in agreement, and I rolled my eyes.

"You're being dramatic." I tried not to smile at the thought of Raven. The last time we had really been together, just the two of us, was right after her Mom's funeral and I was force-feeding her tacos. Shortly after, she went back to Montana for a few months until she learned of the neglect the farm faced and moved back home. Though, hadn't expected to hear from her so soon after seeing her when I picked up the tree with Nan. It was almost awkward enough for me to forget that we had known each other for most of our lives. It also gave me a glimmer of hope. Raven had this ferocity and fearlessness that was so attractive even my preteen-self recognized that I liked her as more than a friend.

I never had the guts to admit that though. I kept every ounce of attraction I felt for her secret throughout our entire friendship. I almost kissed her once in college. She was visiting me, and we were both drunk playing some stupid drinking game. I can't even remember what happened that made us laugh so hard we started crying and clutching our sides. But I do remember the way her brown eyes met mine before they lowered to my mouth. We stopped laughing then, I think I leaned in, or she did. Either way, before it could happen Deserea swung our dorm room door open and stumbled in with her college girlfriend, their lips super glued together.

When the two tripped over a case of beer and dropped onto the bed hard enough for the legs to break we all broke out into laughter that erased all thoughts of kissing. Well, for me, it never went away. Her lips were perfect. A beautiful light brown with a bottom lip that was slightly bigger than her top and formed a heart-shaped pout. I wanted to know what her lips tasted like. I knew they were soft. She had a fear of chapped and dry lips, so she was never without a lip balm.

"Ugh!" I exclaimed, yanking my hand back from the oil that started to spill out. "Son of a bitch." Autopilot had kicked in and I started working on the oil change, but I was not quick enough. I hadn't gotten oil on myself since I first started working on cars.

Deserea was cackling, because of course she was. "Daydreaming about a certain black-haired beauty?"

"You're fired," I murmured, walking to the shop sink. I grabbed a little jar of paste that my Nan made for us and spooned a little bit onto my palm, scrubbing until the oil was gone.

"Come on, Gi! You have been in love with this girl since you knew what a clit was," Deserea said.

"That's disgusting." My lips curled at her words.

Deserea crossed her arms. "Says the lesbian. Regardless, I'm not wrong."

I finished washing my arms and turned to her. "What exactly do you want?"

"I want you to shove your tongue so far down her throat that she forgets how to speak English."

I blinked at her.

"And if you don't do it, I will."

"Is that a threat?"

"Nope," Deserea said, popping the "p". "Just saying that if you don't do it, someone else will."

"Plenty already have."

Deserea shrugged and started walking back to the vehicle she had been working on. "That may be true, but the next one might be the last."

If there are blessings that Colorado bestowed, one was motorcycle weather in December. It was a balmy 63 and a perfect excuse to take the bike out. Never mind that Raven had mentioned on more than one occasion how attractive she found women in leather and on motorcycles. I didn't start riding because of her, but it didn't hurt.

I pulled in front of the little Thai restaurant and parked in one of the three spots available for motorcycles. Another blessing in our little town in Colorado was the different parking spots big enough for trucks and specific for motorcycles. As much as I hated that I had to start a business in a town this small, I loved it just as equally.

I pulled off my helmet and gloves and secured them in the storage case I kept on the back of the bike, running my fingers through my hair. My jacket was a little warm in the blazing sun, but I had been to this restaurant enough times to know how chilly they kept it.

"Gianna!" Ms. Makok exclaimed when the door chimed at my entrance.

I smiled as I bent over to hug her.

"I haven't seen you in so long, sweetie. Where have you been? You can't keep disappearing on us. Next time you wait this long I'm going to go to your shop and embarrass you in front of all your employees and drag you out by your ear." She grinned and tucked a strand of red hair back on my head. "I don't want to drag you by your hair because it's just so beautiful, but if you keep testing me, I will! I see Raven more than you and she has only been back a few months!" She tsked at me. "She's at your usual table. Your drinks are already there," she called as she turned on her heel and walked away.

"Nice to see you, too, Ms. Makok!" I called back. All 4'9" of her was fierce and bossy. Raven and I learned years ago that you don't try to talk when she is talking, nor do you do anything but agree. She's tiny, but feisty. I followed the sound of choked laughter to Raven, who had her hand covering her mouth and was stirring her Thai tea. "Thanks for trying to save me," I murmured.

"You're on your own when it comes to her," she said and turned her head to smile up at me. A surge of satisfaction coursed through me when her eyes trailed down my body. She cleared her throat and met my eyes again, the faintest blush on her cheeks. "Are you going to just stand there?"

I chuckled and took the seat across from her, grabbing her drink. "I missed this place," I murmured when the flavor of the tea settled across my tongue. "I could drink a whole gallon of this and still want more."

Her laugh was a balm on my heart. I hadn't heard her laugh like that since before her mom. "You've done that before. Don't tell me you forgot what happened."

I laughed as the image of Ms. Makok's son, cheering me on as I chugged the tea at this very table over a decade ago, popped into my head. Ms. Makok and Raven took turns holding my hair as I threw up directly after. I am forever thankful that experience did not ruin my love of the best tea ever created.

Chapter Eight
Raven

I did my best to not stare at Gianna when she walked in, but I'm not sure what she was thinking wearing *that*. Not that it was inappropriate for anyone but overly horny lesbians apparently. Her skintight blue jeans, boots, and black/brownish leather jacket that hung over a white t-shirt sent all kinds of feelings through my body. Feelings that someone shouldn't have for a friend, but feelings that didn't give a fuck who was on the receiving end.

When she leaned down to hug Ms. Makok, I decided that those jeans needed to be burned in a fireplace, stat. I would have to make sure she never wore them again because my *fucking goddess.*

Then I got to stare at the column of her throat as her head fell back, and she laughed. I did a good job of hiding my feelings for our entire friendship. I realized I was in love with Gianna when our lips accidentally touched during her last visit. I thought she was going to bite my cheek and I turned my head to yell at her, but instead, our lips brushed. We didn't even have time to consider what happened since someone ran into the room right after. I was terrified that she didn't feel the same way, but those fears transformed from unrequited to requited love after her last visit. I couldn't really say which was scarier.

"How did it go with your Dad?" Gianna asked, holding my drink hostage in her grip.

I rolled my eyes and grabbed it back, a thrill shot through me as I sipped the same straw she just did. I don't know why I acted like it was such a big deal. We had shared more drinks than I could count and always drank after each other, shit, we even shared gum in high school. Though, I don't know why we ever thought that was a good idea.

Actually, I never thought it was a good idea. I think there was a part of me staking claim because it usually happened when there was some other girl around. I was a teenager with a crush. I have matured beyond that. *As I giggle about sharing a straw.*

"Well, he's decorating," I murmured, taking another sip of the tea only to realize it was empty. I glared at Gianna who tilted her shoulder and looked at the menu as if she hadn't been getting drunken noodles for the last 15 years.

"That's good, right?" she asked. "The last time I went over it took two hours to clean. There were take-out boxes everywhere. And all he had was basic furniture."

I grimaced. He told me that Gianna had gone to see him every week over the last few months. I felt guilty, knowing that she took the time to visit him while I floated in a pool of depression. Her hand grasped mine, and my head jerked up to meet her eyes.

"Don't do that," Gianna whispered.

"The regular, girls?" Ms. Makok asked from the counter.

"Yes, please," Gianna responded, not taking her hand from mine. "Don't feel guilty for how you grieve."

"I don't," I said.

"Liar," Gianna quipped with a small curve to her lips.

My own lips lifted in response. "I know I shouldn't, but I feel bad for not being there for him when he needed me."

"Well, he always told me I was a better daughter anyway."

I scoffed and tried to pull my hand away in protest, but Gianna tightened her grip on my fingers.

"He doesn't blame you. He told me that he was happy it was me seeing him like that and not you. You know how your dad is. He wants to be the strong one for you and never wants you to see him weak. It might have hurt him more if you were the one to help him," Gianna admitted. "It wasn't pretty."

I could see the remnants of that mess when I visited earlier today. The fridge was still empty, and I could tell that Dad's head was fogged, but he was better. I thought we were better, until we were hanging up some family photos and he dropped the devastating news on my lap.

"Thank you," I said, trying to hide the shame.

Gianna waved a hand, "You're going to offend me if you say that again. They're my family too, Rav. Plus, you'd do the same for Nan."

I couldn't help the smile that lifted my lips at that. I absolutely would do anything for Nan Margie. "He's doing better, but he put up the most hideous wallpaper."

Gianna laughed so hard and loud that I jumped. Her hand hit the table as her laugh turned into a cackle, and tears streamed down her face. The reason for her laughter hit me like a train and I glared at her even as Ms. Makok put our food down with two more teas. I said thank you, as did Gianna through a gasp. I crossed my arms, pursed my lips, and continued to stare at my so called "best friend" who clutched her side gasping for breath.

"You... you don't like it?"

"What did you do?" I asked calmly as I mixed the rice in with my yellow curry.

"I did nothing. Your dad was so excited when he saw the paper on Etsy."

I paused my mixing to watch Gianna. Her lips were between her teeth as she tried to hold back a grin. "My dad has never been on Etsy."

Her lips popped out of her teeth as the smile widened on her lips. "He has now."

I put my fork down. "Gianna. What did you do?"

She took a large bite of food and chewed slowly, and her mismatched eyes twinkled.

"Gianna Rue McCarthy."

She swallowed her food. "How dare you," she said, affronted.

I giggled and watched her face soften.

"I'm glad you can do that again."

I bit my bottom lip and looked back at my food. I picked up some chicken, potatoes, and rice and took a bite, chewing slowly before I found the courage to speak again. "I'm not sure how long it will last," I admitted. Gianna didn't speak but gave me her full attention. I licked my lips. "Dad wants to sell the farm."

Gianna's eyes went wide. "No," she whispered. I felt the same answer reflected in my eyes as well. When he told me, I nearly punched him in the throat.

"He wants to sell the farm and move to Florida."

"Florida?" Gianna repeated disgusted.

I nodded. "He said that he and Mom talked about moving there when they retired, and he is ready to retire now."

"Why Florida?" Gianna murmured, her confusion matching mine. They never once mentioned Florida in my entire life. Gianna slumped back; her half-eaten noodles forgotten. "How can I help?"

I smiled at that. Gianna knew that I wanted to keep it. She didn't doubt my desire to be close to my mom in a way that equated to me being at the farm. I didn't know if I wanted to spend the rest of my life working there, but I knew that I was not ready to let it go. It had been my parent's dream, and I didn't think that mom would have been ready for that dream to end yet.

"I don't know."

Chapter Nine
Gianna

My mind was whirling when I made it back to my apartment. I was so distracted through the rest of the day by what Raven told me about her dad that I almost forgot to put oil *back* in a vehicle during an oil change. Although the shop was doing well, there would be no coming back after that.

The thought of this town without Moonlight Lake Tree Farm was unimaginable. As was Caswell, Colorado without Raven; however sporadically she visited in the past, if the farm was gone, I knew she would never come back.

As soon as I stepped into my apartment, my cell phone started ringing. I knew who it was, so I took my time closing and securing the door before I answered.

"Hey, Danny," I said as I put the phone on speaker and on the kitchen counter.

"Don't *'Hey, Danny'* me! Where are you?" Danny was yelling over the sound on his side of the line.

I cringed and lowered the volume. "I can hear you fine without the yelling," I said, taking off my shoes and walking to my bedroom. "You said 9:30, it's only-" I glanced at the time on my phone- "nine, I have plenty of time."

"Uh-huh," he said, his voice still louder than necessary. "I was just making sure you weren't going to bail on us again."

"Yeah!" a voice in the background I recognized as Kerri agreed.

I groaned, "Who is us?"

I couldn't tell how many voices were on the other side, all I could hear besides Danny's screaming voice was music playing in the back. Kerri must have been pretty close to Danny for me to have heard her. That was an interesting development that made me smile.

"Just Kerri and me... and Nima, Cassidy, Shay, Lee, and Ale."

My hand froze on the handle of my closet door. "You said it was just going to be you and me, not half of our graduating class!" I argued. Not that it meant much at this point. They were already there, and I would be soon. He was lucky that I even considered leaving my house after 9 p.m. and that was before the guest list multiplied.

Danny laughed. "I invited Raven too, but she said she was working. I'm not sure what she could be doing at nine at night, but whatever."

I knew exactly what Raven would be doing. Trying to figure out how to save the farm from her father. I chewed on my lip as I looked through my closet, pulled out a flannel, a shirt and jeans. My jeans were nearly ruined from work and now I wanted to save them from all potential wear and tear. The look Raven gave me when I was in them did not pass my notice. They were my new favorite jeans.

"Hello, earth to Gi." Danny's voice floated through the speaker.

"I'll be there in 20."

Pete's Bar was owned by our old gym teacher, Tony. We could never figure out why he called it Pete's, and he never told us; I was convinced he had a secret lover he named it after. Danny thought it was named after his father, but his name was Bob. I never heard of Pete being a nickname for Bob. No, there was definitely some long-lost love associated with that name. Maybe unrequited. What a beautiful profession of love, naming a bar after someone.

That's what I should have done, named my shop after Raven. I snorted at myself.

Absolutely not.

She would have hated it.

No, *McCarthy's Automotive* was the perfect name for the shining star of Caswell, Colorado.

I got out of the car service I ordered and headed towards the bar door. I could hardly remember the last time I went out. Actually, that was a lie. The last time I went out was right after Raven's mom's funeral. Raven and I went out and drank so much that I was still drunk three days later.

That was right before rent started getting away from me. The stress of keeping the shop open bled into every waking moment of my life. I was so consumed with how to survive the next few months that I hadn't even let myself out of the house to enjoy any of the nights my friends had invited me to.

Kevin stood at the door and smiled brightly as I approached. "Long time no see, McCarthy!" he said as he hugged me. "Last time I had to carry you out, I know you took a ride-share, but let's not do that again."

"That was post-funeral drunk, Kev. Cut me a break." I laughed.

He pulled away, his hands on my shoulders. "How are they?"

"About as well as you would think."

"Yeah. Well, get as drunk as you want. I'll watch your six." I rolled my eyes, and he threw his hands up. "I know you don't need a man to take care of you, Gianna, but just let me look out for you like friends are supposed to!"

As soon as the bar doors closed behind me, I was attacked by Kerri who screeched in my ear and smelled so strongly of liquor that I was surprised she hadn't drowned.

"Gi!" she screamed. Her brown curly hair nearly suffocated me as she squeezed before she navigated me around the sea of bodies. At some point during our journey, a beer was shoved into one hand and a shot with clear liquid into the other. I didn't have to ask what it was; it was always tequila.

"Gianna!" the group exclaimed as Kerri and I approached.

Danny jumped up and hugged me. "Sorry in advance," he said.

Sorry for what? I mouthed as I was enveloped in another hug. After everyone exclaimed how much they missed me and took the shot with Kerri, I was finally allowed to sit in the vacant chair.

"So how was lunch?" Nima asked in a singsong voice.

I stared at them.

"What? Danny told us that you had lunch with a special person."

"Did you now?" I asked, taking a sip of my beer and glaring at Danny over the glass.

"I might have mentioned that you would be more inclined to come out tonight because you would be in a good mood after going to lunch with a certain bird," Danny said, speaking quickly as if that would erase the betrayal.

"You two have been in love with each other forever, just fuck her already!" Kerri said.

"Oh, you two would make cute kids," Shay exclaimed, her eyes just as glazed as Kerri's, but her voice was soft and dreamy.

I rolled my eyes. I did a lot of that around these people, I might damage a nerve if I kept hanging out with them.

"Your straight mind knows nothing of the queer experience," Nima said, rolling their eyes.

"How do you expect two owners of vaginas to have a child?" Danny asked.

"Biology is only one step in the process of procreation. Having a penis or a vagina can't make you a parent, but love does," Shay said.

Kerri groaned, "Who gave this bitch tequila?"

"You did. You gave her tequila and an edible," Nima said.

Kerri opened her mouth to retort but closed it and pinched her face in thought. "You're right I did."

"What the hippie over here is trying to say is that you need to go for it! You two have been eye fucking each other since high school. And I'm too invested in this relationship to pull my nose out, so don't ask," Danny said, and his hand tapped the table before me.

I blinked to clear the blur from my eyes to see all my friends staring at me. "What?" I asked, feeling self-conscious at the attention.

Danny sighed. "We were just coming up with a plan for you to win Raven."

"Excuse me?"

"It's simple," Nima interjected. "There are three things you need to get your woman."

"You should listen to them, Gi. Three is a magical number, all things happen in three." Shay added.

"She's not my-" I started.

"First," Nima said, raising their voice over mine. "Show her that you know her better than anyone else in the world."

"You have an advantage since you two have been best friends forever," Ale said.

I groaned knowing that he was also in on this silly conversation.

"Second-"

I turned my attention back to Danny.

"You need to show her what life with you could be like."

I frowned. "She knows what life with me is like."

Danny rolled his eyes so hard I thought he might have severed an optic nerve. "She knows what life is like as your friend, she doesn't know what it is to be more."

"She doesn't know what it feels like to wake up to your lips on her skin. To make love to you in the rain, in the snow, or before a roaring fire. She doesn't know what it feels like to be surrounded by a love so pure and true that she will never fear being alone again," Shay said. Shay was always a woman of wistful phrases, but something about those words felt so real.

What it feels like to be surrounded by a love so pure and true she will never fear being alone again. I knew that was Raven's true fear. When that pathetic excuse of a person, Jasmin, forgot how to keep her fingers out of other people's pants, Raven almost lost everything. It was heartbreaking to watch her suffer through that. She thought Jasmin was her best friend, and once Raven found out about the cheating, Jasmin told all of their friends that it was Raven who cheated.

Not that any of them were good friends since they believed Jasmin.

She almost dropped out of school when that happened. I flew to see her, we spent four days drunk and grieving about her lost friendships while simultaneously talking shit about her ex. By the time I left, she wasn't healed, but she was going back to class and eventually graduated. Raven sunk into herself after that. Losing friends after being on the receiving end of betrayal definitely made her less trustful of people. She had friends, but I knew that she had been lonely. It had affected her more than she let on, even now.

"What's number three?" I asked.

Chapter Ten
Raven

I wanted to cry.

I wanted to throw up.

I wanted to cry, throw up, and probably shit myself.

So naturally, I was blaring music just loud enough to distract my thoughts without making me go crazy. Pounce was winding between my feet as I stood in my cabin and stared out the large window. My cabin that I might lose.

I took a large sip of wine and gripped the glass so tightly, I was surprised it didn't shatter. Pounce made a noise and clawed at my leggings. I sat with my feet touching and pulled him into the space between my legs. He spun in a few circles before he laid down and rested his head on my calf.

We both relaxed pretty immediately. His peaceful demeanor helped me which didn't make sense because he had no idea what was happening. Maybe it was just that his cute little head was supported by his cute little paws that all rested on my calf.

Whatever the reason, I needed to keep the tree farm, for both of us. It took until opening day to realize how much I missed being here. There was always work to do during the off-season, making sure the fields were maintained, taking care of the stumps and, worst of all, transplanting the new trees. But I had enough time that I could still be a ranger. Rocky Mountain National Park in Colorado was one of my favorite parks after all.

I should have taken Danny up on his offer to go out. It's supposed to snow the rest of the week and it might have been my last day to drive to town. Normally, I preferred the solitude but at this moment, I wanted a friend. I wanted someone to help me talk through–

Beep. Beep. Beep.

I grabbed my phone from my pocket and smiled at the name lighting up the screen.

> This is what you have left me to suffer alone with

> Why did you leave me alone?

I clicked play on the video and immediately laughed. Shay was spinning in circles with her arms above her head, waving back and forth. The rest of the dancers had given her a wide berth and Nima was jumping on and offscreen, their head thrown back.

> Hahahah! Who gave Shay alcohol?

> ...

> Ah, Kerri. I'm surprised she's not out there with them.

> She's currently mouth to mouth with a girl named Rachel.

> Good for her.

> and a guy named Jordan…

My eyebrows shot up my forehead and I chuckled, "Of course she is."

> Did you talk to your Dad?

> Were your ears burning? I was just thinking about you.

> They were on fire.

> I haven't talked to him again...

> I don't know what to do.

> Did you decide you want to keep it?

> Yeah...yeah, I do. That's why I was thinking about you.

> I thought you might be able to help.

> With my inability to maintain a business I would say no, but I will do anything to get you to plant your roots here with me!

My pulse stuttered, and I reread the message five times. *Plant your roots here with me.*

> Do you know how much he's selling it for?

> I haven't asked him yet...

> Did you tell him you want to keep it?

> No.

> I just sighed, really loudly.

> I probably should have told him.

> Go see him tomorrow and talk about it.

> I'll have to call him, there's a storm coming, remember?

> What's a little storm in Colorado when Moonlight Lake is on the line!!

> I can just call him.

> Yeah, if you're boring.

> You always get more fun when you're drunk.

> I resent that!

> Go home, Gia, you're drunk

> I was waiting to see if you would show up to save me from these people, but apparently you don't care about me anymore.

> You are so dramatic.

I put the phone down to refill my empty wine glass before settling down again with Pounce cuddling himself on my lap. By the time I was halfway finished with the glass a picture came through, and I opened it to see Gianna. Her face looked freshly washed of makeup, her skin still slightly pink. Her hair was wet, and she had a ridiculously big grin on her face. Her mismatched eyes were bright, the corners crinkled. *God, she is so beautiful.*

> I am home!

> Good. Now sleep.

> Um, excuse me! Where's my picture?!

> We didn't have a deal.

> It's always the deal.

I rolled my eyes, but my smile didn't falter as I lifted my phone and angled it to get Pounce in the shot with me. I made a face and took the picture.

> You're so fucking beautiful

I thought my heart might have jumped out of my chest. I bit my lip and read the words over and over again. Gianna had always called me beautiful, it wasn't new, but something about *that* felt different.

> You're drunk.

> That just means I mean it more.

> Goodnight, Gianna.

> See you in my dreams, Raven.

Chapter Eleven
Gianna

"Explain to me how you burned your tree down." I tried to fight the exasperation from my voice, which became exceedingly more difficult, as Nan's laugh filtered through the speaker.

"I don't even know what happened, darling," Nan said between chuckles. "I turned on the lights and the thing caught fire! I think I might have forgotten to water the base."

I thought my molars might crack from how hard I clenched my teeth. Nan had real trees her entire life, all 84 long years. There was no way she *accidentally* forgot to water it.

"We will grab another when the storm clears up."

"Oh, posh. It will just be a dusting. I need the tree tonight. I'm having a party!"

"Have you checked the weather channel?" The news talked about the record-breaking snowfall that was expected.

"Gianna Margaret McCarthy." The panic of my full name made my spine snap, and I sat straight up on the couch. "Since when do you trust anyone else over your Nan?"

"Uh…"

"Never. The answer is never because Nan knows best."

"You're willing to put your only grandchild in danger because you're having *another* house party that requires a tree?" I put Nan on speaker and texted Raven who immediately messaged me back.

"If you leave now, you will beat the storm and see it in your rearview on your way home."

"Raven just said it's already snowing there."

"Guess you should get going then."

"Nan."

"Gianna."

I groaned and dropped my head back. She was going to make me drive the hour trip to Raven's knowing that a blizzard is coming. I am either going to slide off the road and die or get stuck at Raven's for God knows how long.

"Listen, baby," Nan started, and her voice was that soft timber that she knew I couldn't say no to. Manipulative old lady. "I know that you will make it there and home safely. Okay? I really need the tree."

"This doesn't even make sense," I murmured, rolling my eyes at Nan's cheer of victory.

"Not everything is for you to understand, child. Let me know when you leave and when you get there."

"Yes ma'am."

"I love you!" She hung up before I could respond. But I was too preoccupied as I stared at the text from Raven.

> You better not!

I pursed my lips and looked back at the news channel that showed an aerial view of the highway that would take me to Rav...Moonlight Lake. It was overcast but the road was bare, no signs of snow.

> Nan gets what Nan wants.

The drive to Raven's was clear with the snow not starting until I was about 10 minutes out, and in the last two minutes, it was as if someone turned on a snowblower. I ignored the half a dozen calls from Raven because I knew what she was going to say, but I was committed. Committed in my idiocy to make my Nan happy, but also to see Raven. Especially after I told her I was going to dream about her… and then I did.

My hands hurt by the time I parked and let go of the steering wheel. Not snowing for a few hours my ass.

"Are you crazy?" Raven's muffled voice reached me over the howl of the wind as she ran down the stairs of the gift shop. The visible parts of her cheeks were pink from the cold, her black jacket zipped up to her lips, her curls visible beneath her black beanie, and her hands shoved into her pockets.

"Nan," I said with a shrug. Raven stared at me with a furious, but simultaneously soft expression. I had always envied how she managed so many emotions at once. She grabbed my hand and dragged me inside. I could feel the warmth of her, even though both of us were wearing thick gloves.

"Why the hell did Nan think driving through a blizzard was a good idea? I'm going to have some words with that woman. Trying to get you killed," Raven mumbled, ripping the hat off and unbuttoning her jacket to the center of her chest. There was nothing about the act that was particularly sexual, but my mouth was dry, and I could feel my heartbeat in my throat.

I couldn't pinpoint when the change between us started. If there even was a change, or simply wishful thinking. That didn't stop my mind from wandering back to what Nima, Danny, and Shay had said. Three steps that might have been made easier because of the situation Nan had put us into.

Raven raised a brow at me, her beautiful eyes bouncing between mine as she waited for me to talk.

I bit back a smile at her confused look. "She said it wasn't going to happen until after I made it back home, and it wouldn't be an actual blizzard," I said, but the skeptical look that Raven gave me matched my own. Nan had a sixth sense for the weather. She would argue with the weatherman and was always right.

She set me up. That old, conniving, crazy woman.

"Maybe it will lighten up and I can–"

The emergency siren went off on the radio, cutting out a song that I hadn't noticed was playing until now. *"This is Colorado Emergency Weather Services. As of 1600 hours, Central Colorado is in a state of Emergency."* Raven and I stared at each other. *"Blizzard conditions are to worsen over the weekend and into next week with winds up to 60 miles per hour, low visibility, and an expected accumulation of 24 inches of snow. This is expected to last until Monday, December 24th. If you are currently on the roads, seek shelter and safety immediately. This is Colorado Emergency Weather Services..."*

The message repeated as a squeal from the second story drew my eyes up and I watched a little brown body run down the stairs and wind itself through my dripping wet boots.

"That meddling..."

Chapter Twelve
Raven

Was this really happening? It was like a bad dream. Or a really good dream. I watched Pounce weave through Gianna's legs with squeaky abandon.

We were snowed in.

Together.

Fuck.

It crossed my mind briefly that she could make it home in an hour. It was only 4:30, but the snow that had already fallen would make the roads dangerous, and I had no desire to put her at risk. The thought of her being on the road was almost as terrifying as the two of us being locked up together for days.

It wasn't like it was new. It wasn't our first time having a sleepover, but it felt different. Like a shift in the center of who we were. My crush on her never faded, it only grew over the years that I knew her.

"Hot chocolate?" I found myself asking with a grin. Gianna's shoulders relaxed, and she laughed. My heart nearly lurched out of my chest. When she smiled, her whole face lit up, and it didn't matter who you were, you had to smile at the sheer joy on her face. It was the thing that drew me to her when we first met. At nine years old, I knew she was special even if I didn't fully know what it meant.

Even if I didn't know that I had a crush on her from the moment she laughed at one of my stupid jokes. That I was falling in love with her at the age of 10 when she helped carry me home after I flew too high off the swing set and twisted my ankle. Even if I didn't know I loved her at 14 when she came to see me after my date stood me up. She had always been the one person I could talk to whenever I needed. The one constant in my life.

We could be apart for months or even years, and when we were around each other, it was like no time had passed. But this...

This felt different. I was acutely aware of each breath she made, of every ripple of movement, and every blink of her unique eyes.

My mother's passing and the thought of losing the farm had been an awful reminder of the temporary nature of life. With one blink it could all be over, and everything I hoped to accomplish could be ruined. For most of my life, I'd maintained the "one day it will happen" mindset for a real relationship with Gianna.

The accumulation of everything that happened brought me to the realization that *thinking* had become my safety zone. A zone that I lived in to protect myself from disappointment or failure. I no longer wanted to be safe.

I wanted no regrets if I found myself knocking on death's door in 10 hours or 10 years.

I wanted happiness... To be free.

Gianna had reached down to pet Pounce who was rolling on his back and stretching like a cat, luxuriating in the attention.

While one of my biggest regrets was never telling Gianna how I felt, I didn't wallow in the failure to progress into a romantic relationship. Realistically, it was never the right time for us. We were both busy with college and navigating the new world we found ourselves in. I was training to be a park ranger and she was opening a mechanic shop. She was engaged and I was in a relationship. I was hundreds of miles away and she was dealing with the death of her grandpa.

There was always a reason that held me back from pursuing her. Those were all excuses, though. The truth? I was terrified of unrequited love, rejection, and, most importantly, losing my best friend. As far as I was concerned, those were valid reasons to keep my big mouth shut. But not anymore. I had to know if she mirrored some of my feelings. Maybe not love yet, but maybe it could grow.

I turned to grab my gloves from where I dropped them on the counter. We were going to my cabin where it would be just the three of us. Anticipation tickled up my spine. I turned back to where my snowed-in partner was and gasped, tilting back and almost breaking my skull on the edge of a hanging shelf.

Gianna was right behind me. She grabbed my waist to steady me, and my hand went to her arm. I looked up, entranced by her eyes. One blue, one brown. Her fingers tightened on my back, and I swallowed at the sensation. Her eyes went to my throat, up to my mouth and back to my eyes. The way she looked at me was not in what I would consider a friendly way.

Say it. Say it! "That was almost bloody," I said, blinking slowly. *Like an idiot.*

We were trapped together for an unknown amount of time. I couldn't make it awkward by telling her that I was in love with her on day one.

Chicken shit.

When we walked outside, it seemed that there was more snow blowing than there was on the actual ground. The house was cool when we finally made it inside, a cooling warmth that didn't burn as it did in the main building.

Pounce was snuggled firmly against my chest in my jacket. Colorado was not typically the best place to be when you were a warm-weather otter, specifically in winter. In the summer it was almost perfect. Though, he loved the snow. It was almost as if he had been born for it.

"Burr." Gianna shivered. "I'll take care of the fire. If you want to get the hot chocolate started."

I nodded mutely and let Pounce out of my jacket. He ran over to impatiently wait for the fire to start. I watched Gianna pull off her gloves and hat and kneel in front of the fireplace. Her thick legs strained in her jeans, and her hands were a sight to see. The veins were so prominent I dumbly wondered if she drank enough water. She expertly stacked the logs before she looked over at me with a raised brow. I jumped.

"Caught drooling again," Gianna said, the cocky tone in her voice did not go unnoticed. It was both unappreciated and sent nerves of awareness to my core.

I rolled my eyes. "Just wondering if you drank enough water, that's all. Your veins look like they're going to burst out of your hands."

"Looking at my hands too? My, my Raven. You are rather forward, aren't you."

"You wish" was all I could say. I turned around and stomped over to the stove. Her laughter only made my cheeks burn with embarrassment.

That woman. She knew she was attractive and unnervingly charismatic and she loved to rub it in my face. I stirred the boiling milk and dropped in two large pieces of chocolate, continuing the milk tornado I started. A little too vigorous because some chocolate splashed on my face.

I turned to give Gianna a piece of my mind only to be face-to-face with her again. Gianna once again, stood right behind me. This time I only jumped a little. *Am I that distracted?*

"Why do you insist on sneaking up on me?" I asked.

"It is not my fault you're as oblivious as a deaf dog," she said.

I gaped at her. "I am not oblivious, you just tiptoe everywhere." I knew it was a lie as soon as I said it. Gianna always had the heaviest footsteps known to humankind. You would think she was raised by elephants.

Gianna smirked. "You just get so lost in your thoughts that you don't notice anything. It's sweet."

I held my breath as she swiped her thumb on my cheek. Her eyes not leaving mine as she stuck the digit in her mouth, sucking off the chocolate. A little sound of delight came from the back of her throat, and I grabbed the edge of the counter to steady myself.

"Just how I remember," Gianna murmured, her eyes on my lips. She reached around me to grab the spatula off the counter and pressed her body close to mine as she leaned in to stir, preventing the hot chocolate from burning. She was so warm and smelled like fire and all I wanted was to shove my face into her neck. Or nuzzle my face against the shaved side of her head.

The sleeves on her flannel were rolled up, exposing her forearms and the tattoos that covered them. The veins on her arms were just as prominent as they were on her hands.

"You really should drink more water," I whispered. Running my finger along the noticeable vein. She shivered at my touch, and I looked back up. Her pupils were blown, and I realized that I had that effect on her.

"I would, but you're tempting me with chocolate," she said with a chuckle. The sound reverberated deep in her chest, and I struggled to resist the urge to cuddle my face into her just to feel where it started. "Fires started. We should have our own little sauna soon."

I was going to have to dive headfirst into the freezing cold snow... *Maybe the lake isn't too frozen solid for me to shove my head into.*

"Th-thanks," I stuttered. "I'll be there in a second."

She put the spatula down. "You should probably undress. I imagine you're getting warm," she said with a sly smile before turning and walking back to the living room, disappearing from my sight.

I groaned quietly into my hands.

Chapter Thirteen
Gianna

The reality of the moment sunk in. I was snowed in; alone in this cabin with Raven and only one thing popped into my head. *This was my chance.*

I pondered on the three steps that my merry group of misfits had given to me, and satisfaction sat deep in my veins as I threw another pillow down and laid next to Pounce. He had fallen asleep in a small pool I set up near the fire. Not too close to burn his little face, but close enough that the water would stay warm.

I settled myself against the pillow fort I had built using every cushion I could find and threw the blanket over my lap. Raven decorated the space for the holidays, but there was not one Christmas decoration in sight, not that I expected there to be. She was Pagan, so the cabin was filled with decorations befitting Yule. She did have a tree up beside the fireplace; it didn't have the normal ornaments but an array of pendants and candles. It was beautiful.

I leaned back on a "Heathen's Greetings" pillow and grabbed my phone.

> I know what you did.

> I have no idea what you're talking about.

> Are you safe?

> You're an awful liar.

If that was true, you'd be here with me child.

I snorted and rolled my eyes.

> Are you alright?

Takes a lot more than a blizzard to scare this old lady.

> Glad to hear it. Danny is still right up the road so let him know if you need anything.

And how is Raven?

> She's fine. Currently making hot chocolate.

Don't screw this up, Gia.

> Nan.

Don't 'Nan' me, little girl.

> I'm 36 years old.

That's 27 years that you let pass without telling Raven how you felt. Feels juvenile to me.

I gaped at my phone.

> There's not a sensitive bone in your body.

> Normally I would force you to apologize, but I'm sure you will be occupied with the love of your life soon enough.

> You're a nosy old lady.

I rolled my eyes and was about to close the chat when a photo came through. One of Nan smiling…

In front of a perfectly, not burned-down tree.

** *Nan has silenced her notifications* **

I blinked as a mug was placed in my line of sight.

"I remember this one," I grinned. My grandpa gave us matching mugs for my birthday one year. It had a picture of Raven and me on it from when we were 16. Her parents had just bought the farm and we were at the pier that stretched over Moonlight Lake, the farms namesake. Grandma had snapped a photo of Raven and me holding hands. I was looking down at her with a ridiculous grin and she was pointing to something across the lake. Which, once I was able to pull my eyes away from her, I realized it was a deer. How she didn't see how I felt even after that picture, I will never know. Oblivious to the end, my little Raven. If things went well though, she would know soon enough.

"I haven't seen one since that day," Raven admitted, settling into the cushions beside me. She held her feet out to the fire and wiggled her red painted toes. "I think the animals keep them away, mainly the horses. They're assholes if you didn't know. Well, specifically Joe."

I sat up, alarmed, almost sloshing hot chocolate all down my shirt. "Oh shit! The animals!"

"It's okay, they were boarded this morning." Raven laughed. "Unlike some of us who just drive during a blizzard like a wild vigilante, I checked the weather."

I shrugged. "I don't think you're too upset to have me here to keep you safe though."

Raven snorted, coughing to clear the hot liquid in her throat. "Keep me safe? How could you keep me safe when I seem to remember you nearly drowning in snow during the holiday break? I almost had to give you mouth-to-mouth."

I smiled at the memory. Thinking of how my 11-year-old self was so excited to have my first kiss but chickened out because she didn't consent to kissing me. Just saving my life. "I'm sorry you're losing out on sales this weekend," I said, changing the subject. The thought of my lips on hers made parts of my body entirely too interested.

"We have done pretty well this year. I don't think we'll take a hard hit missing this weekend. Plus, it gives me time to figure out what to do about my dad. How about you? This must be the perfect time of year for business, are you doing alright?"

I smiled into my mug. Normally, I hated the sympathy that people had when they heard the shop was hanging by a thread. "Business has been booming actually. I'm not sure what the hell happened, but all month people have been coming in for all kinds of services. Oil changes, engine repairs, tire replacements, even got to work on some motorcycles when the weather was nice."

Raven grinned at me, her cheeks turning a bit pink. "I'm so happy to hear that." She rolled over onto her hip away from me and my eyes dropped to the heart shape of her ass.

Holy shit.

My mouth dried at the view of her ass, and I imagined how soft it would feel. It would overflow in my hands, and I just wanted to take a bite out of it. I looked back towards the fire just as a bottle was brought into my field of vision. A bottle of water. I laughed and looked at Raven to see her self-satisfied grin.

She gestured towards my arms. "You really do need water."

"You know," I started, putting the mug down, "most women would be turned on by my strong arms."

Raven cleared her throat and fixed her sweater. A large scoop neck that drooped down one arm, exposing a shoulder.

"I didn't say they're not attractive. I'm just saying it's a sign of dehydration."

"Is that so?" I asked, deciding to let that revelation sit without response. Instead, I put my hand down and leaned towards her. "How do you know?"

"You pick up a few things when your job is to find lost hikers in the mountains."

"And they look like this?" I tried to keep my voice even as I gestured to my forearm that flexed beneath my weight. I watched her throat work with a swallow.

"Not exactly, but close enough." Her voice was a whisper as she watched my fingers tapping the ground.

"I guess I should listen to the professional then," I acquiesced. I opened the bottle and took a large drink. As she watched the liquid fall onto my mouth, I let my eyes trail back down her throat and chest where a beautiful blush was rising. I wiped my mouth with the back of my hand and closed the bottle, placing it beside my empty mug. "Hungry?" I asked.

Her dilated eyes met mine and her mouth gaped. "Wh-what?" she stuttered.

"Would you like some food?" I clarified with a smile.

This is going to be fun.

Chapter Fourteen
Raven

*T*his is going to be terrible.

Gianna was humming in the kitchen, cooking something that smelled delicious, while I put up the pillow fort since the cabin was now pleasantly warm. Gianna had a habit of singing or humming as she worked, especially when she was cooking, and tonight was no different. She had been a girl of many talents in high school including being in choir. She also wrestled, did gymnastics, was the top in whatever weird mechanic class they had, and took multiple culinary classes.

All of that helped keep her mind quiet. When we first met, she was an angry kid; the loss of her parents at such a young age had confused her, and she hadn't learned how to process her emotions yet. Grandpa was the one who gave her an outlet, and with that, she learned that she was talented in almost everything she did. It's easy to hate someone who is good at everything, but she was always so humble and gracious about it all that it was hard not to love her.

I fluffed the pillows on the couch and created two little nests for us. It was a three-seater, but really it was two since Pounce had his spot on the right side. He loved to sandwich himself between the armrest and the cushion and would become rather indignant if I sat too close to him. I grabbed the remote and started flipping through the streaming services before settling on my favorite.

"Preferences on the dinner movie?" I called.

Gianna's humming turned thoughtful. "Something that will get us in the holiday spirit. I do love my cheesy romcoms," she said back.

"Cheesy rom-coms," I muttered back to myself.

"Yes, Raven. I watch cheesy rom-coms to get the romance I lack in my life."

I smiled at Gianna as she entered the room, a bowl in each hand, before rolling my eyes to cover the pleasure of seeing her act so domesticated. "You could have all the romance in your life, Gi. You are the one who refuses to settle down." I took the bowl graciously from her and picked a movie. One of the few lesbian holiday romance movies anywhere. It was cheesy and set on a farm between a financial tycoon and a farm hand.

Gianna's thigh pressed against my knee as she settled in beside me. I tried to keep my body relaxed even as every piece of my consciousness went to that little contact.

"I'm just waiting for the one I want," Gianna responded. A dimple appeared on her chin as she pursed her lips.

I refused to look at her face. My heart couldn't handle it. I was so hyper-aware that I could practically feel the blood moving through my veins. I felt her gaze on me, burning the side of my face as if someone was holding a fire poker too close.

"Sometimes you can't be too picky if you want romance," I said, shoving a spoonful of soup in my mouth. "This is unfair!" I yelled, gesturing towards the bowl with my spoon. "How are you allowed to look that good, be a great mechanic *and* a great cook?"

Mistake.

I was staring into her eyes; her pupils expanded, and her thigh shifted like a caress on my knee. She smiled softly. Gianna's mascara-covered eyelashes flowed over her cheeks with a slow blink.

"I want to romance my future wife, knowing how to cook seemed to be one of the best ways to do that." She leaned in and I followed suit, drawn to her like a magnet. "I'm also allowed to be picky when I know what I want." Her eyes flicked down to my lips before she turned her attention back to the movie.

My mouth was dry, but the flavors of the soup lingered on my tongue long enough that I was forced to look at the movie and take another bite of soup. Did she realize that she was flirting with me? Was that intentional? I had shoved my crush into a box at the back of my mind to not ruin our relationship, especially after Jasmin. I lost so many people during that debacle that I decided I would never date a friend again.

I wouldn't survive if I lost Gianna and that's what has kept me from pursuing anything further. That and the absolute fear of rejection. I don't think we would have been friends in school if Gianna and I hadn't been neighbors. She was an athlete for Goddess's sake. I was in the back of the school, nursing birds and baby raccoons back to health.

If someone held a gun to my head and told me to recall what the movie was about, I would die. Gianna's thigh was still pressed against my knee even after we finished eating. Her arm rested at the back of the couch, her fingers teasing my hair.

It wasn't an abnormal action for her when we were sitting near each other. She had always been obsessed with my hair. Once I told her that she was allowed to touch it, she dissolved me into goo with the scalp massages. She remained the only person, aside from my hairdresser, that was allowed to touch my hair. Somehow her soft fingers never tangled my wild mane of curls.

It was how we always watched movies, but, as the whole day had been, it felt more... intimate. It felt like *more*. Gianna, of course, appeared completely unbothered by the magnetic pull between us. If it wasn't for her leg that continued to press against my own regardless of how I shifted, I would think I was imagining it. No matter how much I adjusted, her thigh was pressed firmly against my knee. Not that I minded.

Pounce had come out of his hidey-hole and was splayed across both of our laps, asleep. The sun set and the only lights in the cabin were from the TV and the lights I had strung up around the tree and rafters. I could picture our lives like this, Gianna and me. The thought of kissing her right now sent a heat wave right through me, and because of that, I jumped up.

"I'm tired." I practically screamed the words at her.

"Okay," Gianna said slowly.

"My old room is a complete wreck; I've been using it for storage since I haven't had any visitors in a while, so you'll have to sleep on the couch I'm afraid. There are blankets and extra pillows in the cabinet over there. Come on, Pounce." Before Gianna could respond, I grabbed the disgruntled otter and sprinted up the stairs to my bedroom. Not that it put much distance between us since the bedroom was completely open to the room below. I didn't even know why I grabbed Pounce either, as soon as I put him down, he scurried to the stairs.

"Traitor," I whispered at his retreating form. He turned and sniffed at me in disappointment before descending the stairs.

Although privacy was scarce, there was no stopping the pulse between my legs and the need for release. The small piece of seclusion I had made me slide open the drawer at my bedside table. I grabbed the quietest toy I had and imagined my best friend's hands on me.

Chapter Fifteen

Gianna

Raven's reaction that night told me all I needed to know. She felt the charged air between us. It was time to initiate the planned steps. *I sound weird as hell.*

Which was how I found myself setting up a painting station with some supplies I found in Raven's cabin. I had even made her breakfast. But then I was stuck at the bottom of the stairs. *Should I go up to wake her, or let her come down?* She made such an epic escape last night and then had the audacity to fuck herself. She probably thought I couldn't hear her, but those breathy moans that she tried to silence were seared into my mind, and I would go insane if I couldn't hear the full extent of her pleasure and be the one to provide it.

Luckily, my dilemma of just fucking standing there was answered for me when I heard a shuffle from her room. Well, that should take the awkwardness of me going upstairs away. The awkwardness of acting like this was our first sleepover hung in the air though. In the past, I would have jumped on her damn bed and hit her with a pillow until she woke up. That was in our twenties though when the thirties hit, the thought of jumping made my knees ache.

Knowing that she pleasured herself last night brought my thoughts to a halt. How was I expected to act normal after that? In all our years, I had never heard her cum before. I imagined it, often, but nothing in my imagination compared to the real thing. All I wanted last night was to shove my face between her deliciously thick thighs and turn that moan into my name.

I was jolted into action when Pounce started to descend the stairs. I turned to try to find something to occupy myself so I wasn't just standing there like an idiot. I turned to walk towards the kitchen, then turned back towards where the easels were set up in the living room, and then turned back to the kitchen. I would have to ask Raven why she had easels and painting supplies. I had never seen her paint a day in my life.

"Playing ring-around-the-rosie by yourself?" Raven's voice reached me before the sound of her footsteps did.

Playing with yourself? I cleared my throat and turned towards her with a grin as she poured herself a large mug of coffee.

"Hungry?" I asked "I made your favorite." I gestured to the bowls at the two-seater dining table.

Show her you know her better than anyone else in the world.

Something many people didn't know about Raven was that she loved to cook, but she despised making breakfast. She also hated eggs and bacon. Her favorite breakfast being acai bowls. So, I made her one. I topped it with granola, raspberries, blackberries, and bananas. I'm personally a bacon and waffle kind of girl, but she loves them. What Raven wants, Raven gets. Meanwhile, Ms. Piggy was piled on a plate beside syrup and whip cream caked waffles.

"How do you have a body like that when you eat like you do?" Raven asked, eyeing the spread of food. "Thank you."

I grinned as I took the seat across from her. "A body like what, Rav?"

She rolled her eyes and stirred her bowl, ruining my beautiful presentation. I cut a piece of my waffle and brought it to my mouth for a bite only to look up and see Raven's full mouth wrap around her spoon. I shifted, mesmerized as she chewed, her jaw moving sensually. My vision tunneled to her throat as she swallowed.

"This is delicious." Her voice was warped, and her lips formed the words slowly. Her tongue peeked out as she took the spoon into her mouth again. The tongue that I would give anything to taste, even after it has been bathed in her breakfast.

Holy. Shit.

"Do you not like your waffle?"

Raven's question jolted me out of my eight a.m. wet dream, and I shoved the bite of waffle into my mouth.

"Just a little distracted," I responded.

We ate the rest of breakfast in comfortable silence, and when I thought Raven wasn't paying attention, I gave Pounce pieces of bacon. He seemed to understand discretion because he made no movements when I dropped the food, aside from small shifts of his head to grab it.

"What's that?" Raven asked, pointing to the painting station.

I popped the last piece of bacon in my mouth, chewing slowly. "Since we are stuck inside, I thought we might have a little competition," I said.

"Competition?" she asked, her brow raised with a grin.

"Remember that Drunk Painting class we took a few years ago?" I picked up the dishes and strolled to the sink.

"Vaguely," she said.

I snorted. Raven had the memory of the bird she was named after, *long*. "I remember someone being a little butt hurt over how much better my painting was."

"I don't recall it being *that* much better," Raven mumbled.

"If memory serves me right, you walked to the bar, slammed three full glasses of wine, and refused to continue painting," I retorted.

"Sounds childish when you say it like that..."

"There's no other way to say it, dear."

"And I didn't refuse to continue. I was done and wanted to get my money's worth of wine."

I snorted and turned from the clean kitchen propping my hip on the counter. Raven hadn't moved from her seat but had shifted around to watch me. "You sabotaged my painting."

Raven gasped as if I had struck her. "I would never do that!"

"You intentionally bent over and hit my hand with your ass," I said.

"I didn't hear you complain." My cheeks hurt as the biggest grin broke out on my face.

She groaned. "Shut up."

"I thought we could paint your favorite scene," I said, pushing off the counter.

She gestured for me to continue.

"The deer."

Her lips were pulled between her teeth as she tried to fight a grin. *Show her you know her better than anyone else in the world.*

Check.

"That is *not* a deer!" Raven shouted, five hours and many breaks later. "Why does it have a trunk?"

I sat back and looked at the picture. "What do you mean? This is the perfect deer," I said. When did I add gray? I looked down at the paints we split between us.

We don't even have gray.

I looked over to her canvas. "Why is your deer orange?"

"He's sick."

I tilted my head. "Is that why he doesn't have a tail?"

Raven lowered her hand and blinked at the canvas before turning her eyes on me. Our silence dissolved into loud laughter. Pounce started to run around in circles, squealing his laughter. Raven and I fell into each other, her hands gripping mine as we laughed.

We laid like that while our laughter subsided, staring at the horrific paintings together. Though my breath was calm, my heart was a thunderstorm.

"Thank you," Raven whispered, nuzzling her head into my shoulder.

"Thank you for letting me win again," I said. She sat up so quickly I feared she might catch whiplash. "Whoa there, crazy."

"You can't win when you didn't even paint the right animal!" she shouted.

I laughed at her outrage.

"I am clearly the winner."

"We can call it a tie," I said.

"A *tie?*" She stared at me. "This is not a tie!" She stood up and stared at me.

I stood as well, too entertained to keep sitting much longer. It only grew as I looked down at her face pinched with amusement and frustration.

It wasn't until her eyes met mine that I realized how close we were. Her breath quickened as she stared at me. There was no laughter in her face anymore, only hope and apprehension. My thumb brushed a curl from her eye before it trailed down her cheek and pulled her bottom lip from her teeth.

Her eyes dilated and she leaned in, her eyelids fluttering as she anticipated a kiss. My decision had already been made though.

Chapter Sixteen
Raven

She's going to kiss me. I blinked slowly, deliberately. We were so close that if I leaned in a little more, our lips would brush.

"Are you–" My breath caught as her finger dropped to my jawline.

"No, Raven. I won't kiss you," Gianna said.

My mouth snapped shut at those words, and I swallowed before moving to take a step back. Instead, her hand wrapped around my waist and pulled me back into her. I gasped as our bodies fused, every curve of mine fit with hers. Her breath fanned across my face, smelling of bacon and an overwhelming amount of syrup, but somehow, it wasn't unpleasant. My brain didn't care what the smell was, as long as it came from her. Which was really fucking weird.

"You have to kiss me. This starts when you initiate it, not before," Gianna continued. She pressed her lips to the space between my brows.

I closed my eyes and basked in the feel of her lips on my skin.

"Find the courage. Otherwise, this is going to be a long week."

My mouth moved but no sound came out. She wanted to kiss me. I wanted to kiss her. She wanted me. I wanted her.

But as always, my mind wandered to Jasmin. I didn't think that being with her would ruin our friendship. Thinking of her turned my throat to steel, and I stepped back. This time Gianna let me. She dropped her hands and slid them into her sweatpants pockets. Her lips were still twisted in a smile, but there was hurt in her eyes. I wanted to relieve that pain, but a bigger part was terrified of the ramifications of taking our relationship any further.

I had promised myself that I would not live with any regrets after my mom died, but now I wondered what the biggest regret would be. Never telling Gianna how I felt? Or giving us a chance, even if we were doomed to fail?

"Wine?" Gianna asked, the awkward moment flittering past us like the snow that fell on the other side of the window.

I nodded and flopped back on the couch. I would need a lot of wine to make it through the rest of this. I usually had a pretty solid resolve but that had never held around Gianna. She could convince a lion to give up its fur, and I had been on the receiving end of that charisma before. In this situation, I didn't think she would do that, even if I would never rebuke her advances.

"Have you talked to your dad about selling you the farm yet?"

I jumped at Gianna's question, and again when a glass appeared in my line of vision. Pounce sat at the large bay window that overlooked the back of the lake and squeaked at squirrels that ran around outside. I was never sure what he was yelling at them about, but he sure let them have it all the time. From all of my research, otters were not territorial, but then again, most otters wanted to live in the wild and this one refused to leave the comfort of indoor heating and cooling.

"I sent him a text." I grimaced. "Not the way I wanted to go about asking, but I was checking on where he was when the storm hit anyway." I didn't mention that when I said that Gianna was here, and he asked if we were engaged yet.

"Oh?" she prompted, holding up her glass and toasted mine before continuing. "And?"

"He's starting it at 1.2 million dollars."

Her mouth dropped open. "Million?"

I nodded, taking a large sip of wine. "Million."

"Fuck, Raven."

"I know." I texted him while Gianna was cooking us dinner last night and when he told me how much the real estate agent had suggested he list it for, I laughed. Fifty acres of land in the middle of nowhere for 1.2 million dollars. That was way more than my parents initially paid, given at the time it wasn't developed, but it was still an absurd amount.

"I mean, I could sell a kidney, I guess," Gianna said with a shrug.

A burst of laughter escaped me. "Where could you possibly sell a kidney for a million dollars?"

"Are you saying I'm not worth that much?" Gianna pressed her fingertips against her chest, her eyebrows high in offense.

"You're priceless, obviously, but your poor kidney isn't. Plus, I would rather not have to sit by your bedside as you recover from a botched black-market surgery."

"Why do you assume it would be botched?"

"It is the black market, Gi."

A grin lightened Gianna's face but faded quickly. She looked at me over the rim of her glass as she sipped. "Tell him you want to buy it"

"Buy what?" I asked.

"The farm."

"For a million dollars? How do you expect me to afford that?"

"Tell him you want to buy it and ask how long you have."

I stared at her. The thought of trying to get a loan for that amount was insane and, frankly, offensive. I laughed only to keep from crying when he told me.

The number nearly gave me a aneurysm, and I wanted to pretend that I was hallucinating. When I checked his text again a few hours later, the number still glared at me through a gray bubble.

"How am I supposed to come up with that kind of money?" I thought if I asked the question quietly enough it would be like I hadn't said it aloud. But it still felt like a scream in the nearly empty room.

Gianna leaned forward and wiped a tear from my cheek. She had always wiped away my tears. From anger, sadness, happiness, or even if I was just throwing a fit. It sent such a wave of comfort through me that my shoulders relaxed. She held out her hand, and I pulled out my phone and placed it in her palm.

She unlocked it, and I stared at her hands as she typed. Gianna met my eyes before she dropped her thumb to the screen one last time, sending the message and handing back the phone.

I didn't bother reading what she sent, I knew exactly what it said. We chugged the rest of the wine in our glasses, and Gianna filled them again.

"Drunk at two p.m. on a Saturday?" I asked.

"Why the fuck not?" Gianna said.

Chapter Seventeen
Gianna

Mistakes were made last night. The pounding headache told me in not so many words that I fucked up. Three bottles of wine and two hours of karaoke did not a happy Gianna make. When I had that much alcohol, I seemed to forget that I was not 22 anymore. Especially wine. Wine had always given me a headache, but it was as if we were having a house party of two and we just kept going.

The smell of bacon reached my nose, and I floated off the couch and into the kitchen.

"Give me." I sounded like a desperate 90-year-old smoker about to get a fix.

Raven's head turned towards me, and the sense of injustice and attraction flooded me. She didn't look hungover she looked rejuvenated. It was as if she was 17 again. Her hair was out, her curls beautifully coiled around her face dropping down to the middle of her back, and she wore a big grin as she passed me a piece of bacon.

"Have you been possessed?" I asked, tossing the entire piece into my mouth.

"We missed the text from Dad last night because you were plying me with wine, but he said that he would give me six months," she said.

I grinned but regretted the action immediately as the stretch of my face somehow worsened the throb in my head. "Oh god. I'm never drinking wine again."

"Just wine? Not alcohol as a whole?" Raven snorted.

I reached around her, pushing into her space, pinning her to the counter with my hips. I placed one hand on her waist and grabbed another piece of bacon in the other. Her sharp inhale was the only indication she gave that I affected her. I took a bite of bacon and leaned back with a smile.

"Just wine, but now we have six months to get that money together. Piece of cake." I licked the grease off my fingers.

"You keep saying 'we,' but as far as I'm concerned, you have your own business to worry about."

"Raven," the tone of my voice made her pause and look at me fully. "This is my home, too. I helped replace those counters and reface that fireplace. I built the drink stand, I helped paint every room in this cabin, I helped frame the windows, I–"

"Okay! Okay!" Raven interrupted. "I know it's important to you."

"Yes, it is. Is he willing to count this year's sales to the overall price?"

"Why would he?"

"You said that this is the best year that you've had in years."

"Sympathy because of my mom's–"

"Nope. You completely revamped the farm. You stocked inventory with the trees that sold the most. You fixed the wheelchair ramp that has been broken for at least three years, a basic human necessity that was never made a priority! You made it more family-friendly with the sleigh rides, you made it more adult-friendly with spiked hot chocolate."

"Yes, but–"

"Would it hurt to ask?" I asked. Raven had this habit of self-sabotage. Anytime she got on a roll with negative words she would talk herself out of anything. So, I had to interrupt her before she talked herself into a hole that she sat in comfortably.

Raven sighed before taking a bite of bacon and chewed slowly which shocked me enough to shut up, honestly. I watched as she pulled the phone out of her back pocket. After a moment of silence, she put the phone back in her pocket and wrapped her arms around my neck. I grabbed her waist and pulled her closer, dropping my face to her hair. She used the same shampoo since she was 17, the only one she finally found that worked for her curls.

"Thank you," she murmured, nuzzling her head into my chest.

"Grab your computer and let's see what we can do."

"I'm done for tonight," Raven said, and slapped the laptop shut. I didn't envy anyone in finance after crunching that many numbers and reviewing records for the last six hours. It was like having a financial job for the last six hours. My back was killing me, but my headache was thankfully gone. We had the start of a solid plan, and I had full confidence that we could get the money together in six months, maybe even less.

"I know you said you did well, but I didn't realize how well you did this year. That's amazing, Rav," I said, standing from the table.

"We did alright," she said.

"You literally increased profits over sixty percent." I lifted my arms over my head and groaned at the release of pressure. "That's unheard of."

"It's not enough."

"Not yet, but it will be."

"Have you always been this positive?" She laughed.

I shrugged and looked in the refrigerator. "How are you out of soda?"

"I stocked the cabin for one!" Raven said. "I didn't expect to go through everything so quickly."

I raised a brow. "You have the audacity to talk about how unprepared I was for this storm, driving in it, but you didn't stock enough food for the long haul. You're out of almost everything! There's no cheese! No peanut butter, no bread!"

"Looks like a trip to the shop," she said with a sigh, and we both glanced out the large window. Snow was a blur as it blew past and what was settled on the ground was forming mini tornados.

Ten minutes later, we were both bundled up in every piece of cold weather gear that Raven had in the cabin. Pounce, though angry he couldn't come, was pacified with a coconut. I had no idea how Raven was able to keep and store them, but that's why she had an otter while I was petless.

"Ready?" I asked, my voice muffled by the scarf covering my face. I held my hand out to my best friend. She took my proffered hand and blinked her beautiful, big, brown eyes at me. Her scarf was also wrapped around her mouth and nose and her hat sat low on her brow. Her eyes were the only visible part. She nodded and together we stepped quickly out the door.

The feeling was like being pelted with thousands of paintballs all hitting my body at once. The flakes weren't even big, but the pain was. It was an assault on all visible and non-visible parts of my body. I wrapped Raven's hand around my arm, and we dipped our heads pushing through the attack.

Was it even worth it? Did we really need soda? Or milk? Did I really need more clothes? The answer to all of those questions was *yes*. I needed more clothes; I couldn't keep wearing Raven's sweatpants. I had to drop them so low that my ass practically hung out. Though she didn't seem to mind.

What should have been a five-minute walk took about 15. By the time we burst through the doors, our eyelashes were covered in ice.

"Brr," Raven said, as she unwrapped the scarf from her face. "Thank the Goddess the heater still works."

"You always think worst-case scenario," I said, pulling the gloves off my sweating hands. We spent some time filling up our backpacks with some essentials.

I went to grab a bar of my favorite soap from one of the local stores when I saw a flyer on the table beside the soap.

Purchase a service at McCarthy Auto and receive a discounted tree.
Oil change - 5% off
Tire replacement - 10% off
Engine repair - 15% off
Transmission overhaul - 25% off

"Raven," I called. "What is this?"

"What's what?" she asked, turning toward me only to freeze when she saw the bright orange paper in my hand. "Oh. Um, I..." she stuttered. "When you picked up the tree with Nan and told me about the struggle you were having, I figured I had the opportunity to help?"

I walked to her and wrapped her in my arms, lifting her in the air and hugging her so tight the thought of bruising her sat at the back of my mind. I put her on her feet as gently as I could and dropped my forehead to hers, squeezing her biceps.

"You could have the money you need if you hadn't given the discounts," I sighed.

Raven snorted and grabbed my waist. "I still would be short."

"Why did you do that? How did you do that? You don't even know what a transmission is." My eyes searched hers.

"Excuse you, I know what a transmission is!"

"Where is it?"

"It's..."

I snorted. "So, who was it?"

Chapter Eighteen
Raven

"Uh, I did it on my own. The internet works wonders."

I watched as the tip of Gianna's tongue poked out from her lips. Her eyes were on mine, and I could tell her mind was whirling. She pulled her tongue back in and the moisture it left on her lip made my knees weak. Her bottom lip was fuller than the top and I imagined pulling it between my teeth. I wonder what it would taste like, probably sunshine and fucking perfection. Her mouth parted and I saw the pink of her tongue and wondered if it was as warm as she made me feel. I wanted that tongue to touch every piece of me. To feel how strong it was, how much stamina it had because I wanted to pull every inch of...

My thoughts were cut off when she leaned in. *She's going to kiss me. No, she's not. She might, why else would she be leaning in?* I closed my eyes and felt her breath skate across my ear, her mouth touching the shell. I inhaled deeply, the scent of my body wash on her filled my lungs. It smelled better on her.

I felt her mouth move against my ear. Some part of my brain processed that she was speaking words, but I was so focused on the feel of her body so close to mine that I could not decipher the words.

"Mmm," I think I said. I wasn't sure; I couldn't even form a coherent syllable.

Gianna's chuckle was deep and seductive, and I could feel every part of my body respond.

My hands on her waist tightened and against my will, they pulled her closer as my back arched. It was as if my body wanted to swallow her whole. Which wasn't far from the truth. "Deserea said you wouldn't mind," I whispered.

Our cheeks brushed as she pulled back and I started to protest, but her forehead rested on mine. There was a peace I felt whenever I was this close to Gianna. It was why I craved proximity to her even when we were younger, noises weren't always so loud, and my anxiety wasn't always clawing at my throat.

"You saved my grandpa's business, Rav," Gianna voice was hoarse.

"I…"

Her hands cupped my face, and my brain was fuzzy from the intimate contact. All I wanted to do was close the small distance between us. To tilt my head up and meet the pillowy soft lips with my own.

Gianna licked her lips and pulled her bottom lip into her mouth. I could see that she wanted to kiss me, and for a moment, I couldn't understand why she didn't.

You have to kiss me. This starts when you initiate it, not before.

Oh yeah. That's why.

She kissed my cheek. "Let's get what we need and get out of here."

We grabbed the necessities before trekking trekked back to the cabin where we were greeted by an excited Pounce. He was waiting at the door for us to return, and once we stepped inside, I gave him a vine of grapes that I had stored in the shop. He sprinted to the fireplace, his head lifted high to not drag the grapes on the floor.

Gianna walked over to start a fire, and I went to pour us some wine. She had been my best friend long enough for me to know that, though she claimed to be done with wine, she wasn't. It was her favorite beverage aside from Dr. Pepper and Thai tea. The temperature had dropped, and we returned right before the wind started to whistle. I had never been more grateful for the cabin while it showed such resilience to the blizzard.

Electricity had not gone out yet, and even if it did, we had three large generators that could provide power for months.

I never meant for Gianna to find out about the flyers. I wanted to help, and I knew it was the time of year when people were looking for any kind of deal they could get. If they could pay for an oil change and get a discount on a tree, they would. Especially since trees were not the cheapest.

I walked into the living room with two glasses in time to see Gianna and Pounce playing with a furry cat toy. A soft jazz instrumental played, and candles flickered from around the room. It wasn't late in the day, but the sky was shadowed, and the sheer amount of snow seemed to block out the light. It was so romantic that I almost ran away.

"Here you go," I say, passing the glass to her. Gianna smiled up at me and I swore the divine appeared.

"Thank you, darling," she said. *Darling.* She took a sip with an appreciative hum and placed it on the table before placing my drink beside hers and standing. Before I knew what was happening her hand was extended at me. "Will you dance with me?"

Dance? I looked around. "Where? Here? Now?"

"Do you have somewhere else to be?" The curve of her mouth was enough to turn me into a puddle, and I shook my head.

My mouth was too dry to respond as I placed my hand into hers. Gianna grinned, closed her fingers around mine, and pulled me up before her other arm wrapped around my waist. I grabbed her back and followed her lead as she glided across the living room to the beat of the music. Our bodies were so close there was not even enough room for air between us. I wondered if she felt the race of my heart. She was so warm and her arms around me and my hand in hers felt like completing a puzzle. That was what it was like being with Gianna. I never felt incomplete without her, but being with her added so much more to me. I was always better with her; I felt happier, lighter.

"Do you remember the first time we danced like this?" Gianna asked with her cheek against mine, her voice husky in my ear. "I think that's when I first realized what you meant to me."

The blood in my ears beat in time with my heartbeat.

"It was right after Tiffany stood you up, I came over with vodka–"

"It was definitely tequila." I interrupted.

"I came over with tequila," she laughed. "You were supposed to go to a party, but we stayed in and had our own party instead. Then, you decided you were so mad about being stood up that you burned every note you ever received from her and nearly burned the bathroom down."

I reared back. "I seem to remember burning them in the bathroom was your idea."

"Because you wanted to start a fire in the plastic trashcan in your room. If we were going to have a fire, best to have it where the water is."

I raised a brow at her but resumed my position. She wasn't wrong. No one should mix tequila and fire, especially after watching an action movie where they use alcohol to spit fire. They must have firefighters on set because that shower curtain went up like a fuse.

"Before we saved your house from a fire, we danced. It was the first time I got to hold you like that. Then, during my first trip to see you at college, we shared another dance. That was the when I realized you controlled me every time you walked into a room. Every roll of your hip was a rush I never knew I was missing," Gianna said.

I could almost smell the sweat and bile as the memory flashed in my head. We were this close during that dance, but it was nowhere near as tame. It was right before Jasmin and I got together, Gianna was fresh off a break-up and all of my college friends, including Jasmin, were pushing me to be with her. They could see something I refused to see at that moment. I could still imagine the feel of her against my ass. I could remember how tightly she wrapped her hands around mine, holding them to my stomach and rolling her hips with mine.

"The last dance was my favorite though." Gianna grabbed both of my hands and put them around her neck, her fingers caressing the back of my arms as she lowered her hands around my waist and pulled me even closer. I leaned back to meet her searing gaze. She smiled and ran a finger down my cheek, I had to close my eyes at the sensation. The feelings in my heart and body were overwhelming.

Our last dance was 10 months ago when she came to visit me, right before my mom died. I took her out to dinner at the fanciest restaurant I could afford, which wasn't a lot since I had just moved, and it was even more difficult and expensive to find a place that allowed a pet otter. After dinner, we went to a little pub that was around the corner from my house and we ended up dancing. We were those annoying people who, no matter what song was playing, were swaying like teenagers on prom night. We would stop, have a drink, and just start dancing again. I thought that I was going to profess every stupid feeling I had for her right there, but fear got the best of me.

"That was when I realized that no matter how long I try to deny it, no matter how hard I try to fight it, you were it for me. I wanted to be the one you reached for in the morning, the one you came home to. I wanted to be the one who helped you take care of Pounce, to be the one who picked you and your drunk friends up and who you fell into bed with because you couldn't keep your hands off of me. I wanted to be the one who held your heart in my hands and cherished it like you deserved," Gianna said.

I tightened my arms around her neck. "What are you saying?"

Gianna stopped moving and brought both of her hands to my face. She leaned in so close that her lips touched mine with the next words she spoke. "I'm saying, baby girl, that I'm going to break my promise of you being in control of this if you don't kiss me right now."

For the first time in years, I didn't consider the potential consequences or the risk of losing the one person that meant the most to me in the world. I didn't think of anything but her as I pressed my lips to hers.

Her lips tasted like wine with a hint of chocolate and raspberries, and I could not get enough. My hands tightened around her neck, and I stood on my toes, pressing myself even closer. One of her hands dropped to my lower back, her fingers tickled over the curve of my ass as she pulled me into her.

Chapter Nineteen
Gianna

Raven's lips were better than I could have ever imagined. She didn't believe in God, Heaven, or Hell, but she believed in what she called Divine. If the divine could be bottled, that kiss is what it would taste like. The apotheosis of everything we worked for, everything I fought for. Every question I ever had was answered with her kiss.

Raven's lips parted and I took the invitation for what it was and pressed my tongue into her mouth. Her moan spurred me on even more and my hand on her face moved to grip the back of her neck pulling her closer. I wanted to devour every part of her, to cover any other touch and erase every wound, especially the ones caused by women who were less than worthy.

I wanted to wrap myself so tightly into her that we wouldn't know where she ended and I began. I wanted to embed myself into her soul. I knew she craved me like I did her. I knew she wanted me, but I wanted her to admit it aloud. Raven refused to ever admit that she was anything other than "okay."

Step two, let her see what life with you could be.

With her, life would be easy. This was what I would give her, all of me for as long as she would have me, which I would not accept anything other than always.

I kissed her mouth, her cheek, and the space between her eyebrows before I dropped my forehead against hers. I could have lived in that space forever with her, the space we carved for us.

"Wow," Raven whispered and pressed her lips to mine again. I chuckled and traced the side of her face, reveling in being able to touch her this way and how she leaned into it.

"I don't know why you waited so long to kiss me. I could've blown your mind years ago," I joked.

Raven didn't respond, she just rubbed her nose against mine and held me close.

As much as I wanted to take Raven to bed that night, I knew her well enough to know that she needed time. If we rushed, she might not have regretted it, but it would have set us back on whatever progress we had made so far. Though, I did smile at the thought of her being awake most of the night tossing and turning and probably a wet mess.

I had forced her to go upstairs without me but with a promise to make it up to her. Depending on how she came down those stairs would dictate the tactic I took. I was never one to take the shy route with anything I did. Well, that wasn't true. It may not have been the shy route, but I always took the cautious route with Raven and her feelings. She was a chronic overthinker, and any adjustment to her normal routine ended up throwing her off completely.

I never held anything back from her as my best friend, but my feelings that extended beyond the friendly type were handled cautiously. The points where we were almost more but never crossed the line, I never brought up outside of the moment. Raven was quite skittish, and I knew the thought of having another relationship with a friend terrified her. Even if that friend was me and I would rather gnaw off my left foot than hurt her.

I didn't know if we had actually taken a step forward, but I sure as hell didn't want to go back. I wanted to keep this small bit of momentum we had and push it forward.

I had planned to wake up and give her the biggest "I don't expect anything, but I would love if something did happen" face.

"Gi," a soft voice whispered in my ear and a gentle hand rubbed my arm. I was on my back, leg thrown over the back of the couch, and the blanket half off my body. Only one person had ever woken me up that sweetly and to hell with not expecting anything. I reached up and wrapped my arm around Raven's waist, pulling her on top of me. Her squeal of laughter went right to my heart and a smile to my face.

All the subtlety of a gunshot.

"Good morning," I murmured through a mouthful of her hair.

"Wait," she laughed, pushing off of me. "Come here!" She struggled up and pulled me to my feet, rushing me to the window. "Look."

I followed the point of Raven's finger to the tree line in her backyard. The snow had slowed but still fell in large sheets thick, on the ground like a fluffy cloud. A large animal stood just visible through the trees, and I rubbed my eyes to clear the sleep.

"Is that a..."

"Deer!" Raven squealed. "I think the snow covered the scent from the animals, and so they might be coming back."

I met her bright brown eyes with a raised brow. "Rav, darling. You work as a Park Ranger–this is not your first deer."

She rolled her eyes. "I know, but I haven't seen one at the farm in years! I love blizzards!"

I was inclined to agree but for completely different reasons. My eyes trailed down her body to her bare legs. She was wearing a large shirt and a very tiny pair of shorts. I could just see the line of black beneath the hem of her shirt, and my mouth dried. The desire to fuck her only intensified with each movement she made, her thighs and calves flexed as her shirt lifted.

Raven turned to pull me closer to the window. I stumbled, and she put her arm around my waist, resting her head on my chest. Pounce stood on his hind legs staring at the creature outside, his interest just as peaked as Raven's. I dropped my arm around her shoulders, kissed her hair and dropped my head onto hers. I didn't know how long we stood like that, but with each passing moment, the urge to kiss her grew.

"Truth or dare?" she asked.

I blinked and pulled back.

Her lip curled into a wicked smile when she met my gaze.

"What?" I asked the grin on her face reflected on mine.

"Truth or dare." The last time we played this silly little game, we were in a cabin in Rocky Mountain National Park, and I ended up running naked through the yard into a stream where I had to submerge myself and run back. It would have been fine if a porcupine hadn't decided it also wanted a midnight swim. I still had a scar on my ass cheek where a quill got me too deep.

Even knowing that night ended with Raven leaning over my bare ass laughing as she pulled out quills, I still found myself saying, "Dare."

"I dare you to answer honestly to everything I say in the next 60 seconds."

I couldn't tell if my heart skipped a beat, sped up, or stopped pumping blood entirely. Her grin faded, but the corners of her eyes were still crinkled with the hidden smile.

"Do you want to kiss me?" she asked.

I wondered where this side of Raven had come from. Maybe it was because of the friendship we had locked in so tightly had blinded me to how bold she was in relationships. The face she showed the world was not nearly this forward. "Yes." I tried to put confidence into my one word, but it came out a broken whisper.

"Do you want to fuck me?"

I blinked rapidly at her. *Who the fuck is this woman?* "For years."

She shuddered. "Why haven't you tried?"

"Because I would never want to make you uncomfortable."

"What if I said I wanted you to kiss me? *And* fuck me?" The words were barely out before I jumped on her. It was as if I was a needy teenager again, kissing my crush. My hands were everywhere, and I swear I sucked both her lips into my mouth. It wasn't sexy but her eagerness was. She responded with the same enthusiasm, her hands everywhere.

"Truth or dare," I asked against her lips.

"Dare."

"Take your clothes off."

Chapter Twenty
Gianna

It was like a dream.

The sunlight streamed through the windows. The white blanket of snow was bright, and fresh snow still fell, covering the trail from the deer. The light hit Raven in a beautiful halo, her naked body like a painting. She laid on a blanket on the ground before the large window.

"What are you looking at?" she asked. Her chest moved so rapidly with each breath that I feared she might hyperventilate. And that made me smile.

"Admiring the view," I said, moving closer to her.

"Why…" She swallowed as I dropped before her, running my hands up her legs. She was softer than I imagined, my hands gliding across her skin like silk. "Why are you still dressed?"

"Because you didn't dare me to take my clothes off, and now it's too late. I get to have my wicked way with you first," I murmured.

"But I want to–"

I tsked and straddled her hips. Her pupils dilated, leaving only a small circle of brown around them. I grabbed her hands that rested on my thighs and placed them above her head. "Grab the blanket." She did and I took a moment to fully appreciate the way her breasts lifted. I always loved them. Not too big, but enough for a large handful, her nipples a perfect brown and hardened. Raven's back arched as I dragged my hands down her arms and dropped them to her breasts.

"Tell me, how do you like it?" I leaned down and took her nipple between my teeth, biting gently. "Would you like my mouth or fingers?" I switched to her other nipple and my thumb traced the other. "Do you want me inside of you?"

She gasped as I pulled her nipple between my teeth. "Pe...pen...penetration does nothing for me."

"Mm, noted. Anything else?" I murmured, my lips finding their way to her neck. I sucked at the soft skin and her hands dropped to my arms.

"No... no," she groaned as my fingers tickled across her stomach.

"There's no reason to lie or be embarrassed."

Raven closed her eyes.

"I'm going to learn every part of your body, everything that makes you whimper, scream, cry, and beg for more regardless." I leaned over her and took her bottom lip between my teeth before kissing her.

Her lips were perfect, they melded with mine as if they were made for my kiss. Raven pushed her tongue inside my mouth, and I melted into her. It was easy to get lost in her kiss, in her gentle touch, in everything that was Raven. I couldn't help myself anymore, foreplay be damned. My hand dropped to feel her pussy, and I groaned. "You are so wet." My shirt started to rise, and I pulled back letting her remove it to reveal the black sports bra I wore. It would be cleaner anyways. I rolled off of her onto my back and looked at her expectantly.

"What are you doing?" she asked.

"Sit your pretty ass on my face, baby girl. I want to see how you look riding it."

She gaped at me, a flush rising to her cheeks. "I'll suffocate you! Do you see the size of these thighs?"

"If I die eating out your sweet pussy, I will have tasted heaven even if I go to hell. Now come here."

I quirked a brow at her as she continued to stare at me. Raven sat up before slowly placing her legs on either side of my head, sitting on my chest.

"Are you sure?" she asked tentatively.

Instead of responding, I grabbed Raven's thighs and forced her over my face. My mouth wrapped around her clit. A combination of her surprised sound and the taste of her sent a wave of pleasure down my spine. Raven's fingers clawed into my hands that were wrapped around her thighs, and her head fell back. I explored her pussy with my tongue, and I would never get enough of her taste. If I woke up tomorrow to find out this was all a dream, I would do whatever I could to have my mouth on her again to see if it was as good as I dreamed.

The sound of her moans were distant because of how tightly her legs pressed against my head, but I didn't care. I would hear it plenty later when I had her on her back, her side, her face. At that moment, I wanted her to fully submit to the pleasure that I would work from her body. I wanted to taste every part of her.

Raven's back was arched, and her chest pushed forward, the light illuminated her dark skin in gold. She was magnificent in her pleasure, especially when her hips started to grind against my tongue.

I rubbed my thighs together to relieve some pressure, but it wasn't enough. If I had any desire to distract myself from what I was doing I might touch myself, but I was utterly focused on the beautiful woman above me who was dripping down my chin and tasted of heaven.

"Gianna–" she whimpered. "Don't stop, please don't stop."

As if I could if I wanted to. I wanted to see her lose control, to feel her body tremble with release. I didn't have to wait long; her body convulsed, and she shook with a loud moan as she came. But I didn't stop, I wanted to drink her clean. Raven tried to close her legs, her hips shifted away from my mouth, her hands pushed against mine as she tried to pull away.

"I can't," Raven said, falling onto her back to unlatch my mouth from her.

She hadn't told me that she could only handle one orgasm at a time, so I was going to continue until I got at least one more.

I sat up, my hands on her ass, elevating her so that I could continue to devour her. The noises Raven made enticed me further, they were fucking addicting. I wanted to pull every sound that I could from her. I watched her face transform into pure pleasure. Her eyes were closed, and her hips rolled against my mouth again. I worked to coax her to the edge without overpowering her sensitive clit.

"Oh god," she moaned and clenched as another orgasm rolled through her body. Her legs squeezed my head so hard I feared she might actually break something. I relented to her pleas and placed one last kiss before pulling away.

"You're beautiful," I whispered, kissing her thigh. "You taste so good." Raven's dark gaze met mine, and her mouth parted as I licked my lips. "I could listen to you cum every day for the rest of my life." I trailed my lips up her legs, stomach, and breasts until I lay fully on her. I kissed her, shoving my tongue into her mouth. I wanted her to taste what I did, to know why I wasn't able to stop.

"You are a menace with that tongue," Raven said, her voice deep with satisfaction.

"Just wait until you see what I can do with my fingers," I teased, kissing her nose. Her legs wrapped around my waist and flipped me over until she was straddling my hips. I blinked up at her, surprised.

She grinned, leaned down, and licked the shell of my ear. "Wait until you see what I can do with my fingers."

I clenched at the thought as her hands dropped to the waist of my sweatpants and pulled them off. My briefs followed. I had never seen Raven so comfortable with being naked. She thought not being as thin as our classmates was a disadvantage, but every inch of skin she had was beautiful. At that moment though, she was the most confident I had ever seen her. Each move of her sliding down my pants made her breasts sway and her pussy still glistened with her orgasms. I hated that I waited so long to take her, but now that I had, I never wanted to let her go. I would do whatever

I could to erase the idiocy of her ex and how she utterly destroyed Raven's trust in friends turning into lovers. Raven was everything to me when we were best friends, now that she was almost mine, I refused to lose her.

I sat up and removed my bra, leaving myself naked to her and crossed my arms behind my head. She sat on my shins and stared at me, taking in every piece of ink that covered my skin, every bruise, freckle, and dip. Her eyes were like a caress as they explored my body. My nipples were stiff, and my clit throbbed so painfully I might cum if she breathed on me too hard.

"Wow," she said.

I smirked. "Enjoying the view?" She didn't come back with a snarky reply, she just laid on me. The feeling of our naked skin together was like coming home. Her body fit with mine, her soft skin like butter. Her tongue ran up the valley between my breasts and she took a nipple in her mouth as her fingers dropped to my pussy.

"How do you like it?" she asked, teasing my nipple with her teeth.

I groaned at the feeling of her mouth and fingers as she strummed them along my clit. "I like it all," I murmured, tracing my hand around her face.

She leaned up and kissed me just as her fingers pushed into me.

"Fuck," I groaned, my back lifting. Her thumb met my clit as she pushed in and out of me. She rotated and pumped slowly and quickly, before curling her fingers in a way that made me see stars. She studied my face with each change she made, gauging what I liked and didn't.

Raven settled into a rhythm that drove me insane. She kept me at the edge of pleasure without letting me go. The way she kissed my mouth, sucked my neck, bit my nipples, overwhelmed me with feelings. Her mouth met mine again just as the pressure in my core hit a crescendo. She swallowed my moans as if she wanted to be the only one in the world to hear what she did to me.

Chapter Twenty-One
Raven

Gianna and I laid facing each other in front of the fireplace, naked and cuddled together in the fuzzy blankets. Her eyes bore into mine with an intensity that made my breath falter. She held one of my hands against her chest while the other brushed along my hip, the softness of her touch pleasantly tickled my skin. Gianna's blue and brown eyes were soft and whirled with emotions that I knew were reflected in my own. A thought that both terrified and thrilled me.

"Now what?" I asked. I don't know why I interrupted the beautiful bubble of silence we had going, but the way her eyes widened and the smile that lit up her face caused me to immediately roll my eyes. I should have known better.

"Are you asking me what we are?" she asked. "Oh, I don't know. This is just all so fast, so sudden."

"You're annoying." I groaned, dropped onto my back, and covered my eyes.

Gianna chuckled and rolled on top of me, supporting her weight with her hands as she rubbed her nose on mine. "I'm also yours," she whispered. She kissed my nose and cheek. "I have always been yours, baby girl. I was just waiting for you to catch up."

I scoffed. "Is that so? Does that mean your engagement was just a rouse?"

"Hm. You're right." Gianna kissed my nose. "There were lulls in my judgment, but I knew since the moment you flew off the swing in fifth grade and broke your wrist that you were the one for me."

"It took me breaking a wrist for you to decide I was the one?" I asked raising my brow.

She nipped at my nose. "It took you swinging that casted arm at Mary Ann when she called me a fag for me to realize you were the one."

"I really hated that girl."

"Didn't we all? But the fact that you were willing to risk suspension or even jail time for me was everything."

Luckily, my swing didn't land, and it didn't result in juvenile detention or anything else unsavory. The principal was able to dissuade Mary Ann's parents from seeking punishment when he had his partner bring him lunch during their meeting. That was the day the school found out he was gay.

"I didn't ask what we are, Gia. I asked what now," I said, trying to avoid the conversation of my less-than-stellar school record.

"Well, are you hungry?" she asked.

I rolled my eyes again. "That's not what I mean!"

"Do you even know what you mean?"

I pursed my lips. Nope. I had no idea what I meant. I might have meant what was the next step for us, or maybe I was hungry, or maybe I wanted a shower, or to taste her again. Or what happened if we did decide to give this a shot and it didn't work and I lost my absolute best friend? What if we ended up hating each other? *What if we ruin everything?* I had been down this road before with Jasmin. She left me with nothing, she took all of my friends and I almost failed out of college. If it hadn't been for Gianna...

The feeling of Gianna's lips on mine pulled me from an impending panic. She dropped to her elbows, rested her forehead on mine, and took a deep breath. I grabbed the back of her neck to keep her as close as possible. Her all-consuming presence and the gentle beat of her heart steadied me until I was able to calm the anxiety that clung to my chest like a vice.

"You know," Gianna said, her lips trailing up the side of my neck and her thigh pressing into my center. I arched into her touch. "I've never been one to back away from a challenge." She continued to move her thigh rhythmically against my pussy and heat flared in my core. "I usually go after what I want." She dragged her teeth down my jaw, ground into me, and my thigh moved against her in response. "I've wanted you for years, Raven, and I don't plan on giving you up. Ever."

My body throbbed at her words,

"You're mine," she panted. Her arousal coated my thigh, and I couldn't find it in me to care past the pleasure coasting up and down my spine. "Say it. Say you're mine."

I would have told her the sun was made of ice and the oceans were made of roses if she asked, as long as she didn't stop doing what she was doing.

"I'm yours," I whispered.

Chapter Twenty-Two
Gianna

"You know your bed is much more comfortable than the couch," I said with a stretch.

Raven smacked me with a pillow. "I knew you only wanted me for the bed."

"It's a very comfortable bed." My voice was muffled by the pillow, but it smelt of her, so I didn't remove it. Pounce wiggled his way up the bed, lodged himself between our bodies, and flopped onto his back with his paws waving. "See, he agrees." I laughed and scratched his belly.

"Go make me breakfast," Raven yawned. She wrapped her arm around Pounce and pulled him into her, he snuggled his face next to hers and my heart did a funny flip at the sight. Raven had always had a soft spot for animals, so when she chose park ranger instead of veterinarian, I was surprised. When I asked her about it, she said she didn't want to charge money to help fix animals.

"What do I get if I make you breakfast?" I asked, propping my elbow up and resting my head on my fist.

"My undying appreciation," she said, leaning her body towards me.

"I don't think that's nearly enough for my culinary skills," I responded.

She leaned closer, the corner of her bottom lip disappearing between her teeth. "A kiss?"

"Tempting, but I need more."

"What would you like?"

I brushed my lips over hers. "How about. You owe me one."

Her chuckle was a whisper across my lips. "What would I owe you?"

"One favor, whatever I want."

"That sounds like a big payment for some food."

I pressed my lips to hers in a gentle kiss. "Say yes."

"Yes."

"Good." I stood and put on a pair of "Moonlight Lake Tree Farm" sweatpants and one of Raven's shirts. I would have to turn the heat up; it was so cold in the cabin I might freeze my left tit off. It was my favorite side so I had no doubt it would be the first one to go.

I leaned over Raven to give her a quick kiss, but she held me in place. Her lips enticed mine, and I dropped to my knee beside the bed. Raven's tongue pushed into my mouth, and the moan escaped. I had spent most of my life imagining what it would be like to be able to kiss this woman whenever I wanted. And now that I have tasted her lips, I would hold onto the ability with both hands. I knew Raven better than I knew myself. I knew how beautiful life with her could be and I needed to make sure she didn't psych herself out before we could discuss the next steps.

A loud grumble broke our kiss, and I laughed. Raven's head dropped to the pillow, and she covered her face with her hands, embarrassed.

"That's not even the loudest sound I've ever heard your body make." I chuckled.

Raven waved her hand and shooed me away.

When I finally made my way downstairs with Pounce hot on my heels, I immediately went to the thermostat. *Sixty-four degrees!* Absolutely not. I adjusted the gauge and moved it to a perfect, 70.

I went to the kitchen and started cooking, appreciating the warmth from the stove. The bacon was sizzling on the stove when Raven finally came down the stairs. I checked the hash browns in the oven and closed it to see Raven at the thermostat.

"I already turned it up," I said dropping the oven mitt on the counter.

"Did you? It says it's 63 degrees in here!" Raven shivered as she adjusted the temperature.

"I just turned it up to 70 because it was 64."

"Shit," Raven said.

"Why shit?"

"You just keep cooking, and I'll see what's going on with the heater."

I felt indignant at the thought of her going to fix the heater when I had more expertise. I'm a mechanic for fuck's sake. I wiped my hands on the rag and tossed it on the counter.

"Keep watch on the hash browns and I'll take care of the–" I stopped short at the look on Raven's face. Sometimes I forgot how independent she was. I could be holding a lighter and she'd insist on rubbing two sticks together instead. "Fine." I held my hands up in surrender. "I'll let you do it."

Raven approached me and wrapped her arms around my waist. "You know me well enough to know that I want to do it myself, but not well enough to not ask in the first place."

"Baby girl," I started, resting my hands on the delicious curve of her ass, "you don't know me well enough if you don't think that I'm going to try to help in any way I can."

"I know, it's one of my favorite things about you." Raven kissed me and was bundled up in snow gear and out the door before I could tell her to stay warm.

Fifteen minutes passed before I started wondering where she was. I turned off the oven but left the food in there to stay warm before I moved to the window over the sink to see where she was. When I didn't see her, I walked over to open the front door when movement at the large window caught my eye.

There she was. In the back of the house, where we had seen the deer, with an ax in her hand. I stood in awe as she started chopping large pieces of wood. In all my years of knowing Raven, what she was capable of before she became a park ranger and after going their grueling training, I still wasn't prepared for just how strong she was. I stood in awe as she started chopping large pieces of wood.

That woman had saved dozens of lost, hurt hikers and homeless people from four different national parks. She was a badass, there was no doubt about it. But I had never seen her work like that.

I had only felt gay panic a few times in my life, but they all paled in comparison to watching Raven. Her jacket was off, a long sleeve black shirt hugged her body tightly. Large chunks of snow fell around her as she swung the ax and split a piece of wood in half.

Thank the gay Gods for Raven.

I didn't even think as I threw on a jacket, boots, a hat, and gloves. Pounce followed me out the door. He squeaked happily as he bounced around in the snow trying to catch the snowflakes that fell. He was adorable, and I had no idea how he was even able to stand the chill.

"This is the sexiest I've ever seen you," I said, approaching Raven as she set up another piece of wood.

"Are you just going to stand there and drool?" Raven grunted as she sliced the piece in two. I took an axe from the small container that sat beside a shack and grabbed a stack of wood.

"I thought you 'prepared for the storm'," I mocked. "I seem to remember you being out of sorts when I got here, and you yelled at me for driving."

"Yes, well, I was prepared for five days with the heat." She swung again. "Not ten days, two extra mouths to feed and the heater going out."

"Two?" I grunted swinging the axe. When the blade contacted the wood, my entire arm vibrated at the impact. My teeth chattered and my body ached immediately. "You didn't plan for Pounce?" I tried to keep my words light, but I could hear the strain in my voice. It was well worth the sense of accomplishment I felt... until I looked down and saw that I had cut only a small sliver.

Raven chuckled and cleaved another piece in two, the ease with which she did it was equally irritating and arousing. Was it normal to get turned on by someone chopping wood? All I wanted to do was peel Raven out of the leggings that hugged that delicious ass and bury myself between those full thighs, and maybe this time, I would drown or suffocate.

One could hope.

I knew Raven was speaking and from the look on her face, I could tell it was something I should be offended by. Yet, I could not find a single fuck when her body called me like a siren. Raven was startled when I wrapped my arms around her waist. I don't even remember walking to her, just the feel of her warm body in my hands.

"I think that's enough, wood." I rasped.

Chapter Twenty-Three
Raven

Pounce was right on our heels as we stumbled back into the cabin, wood piled into our arms and my jacket still outside collecting snow. Gianna and I placed the wood on the rack beside the fireplace before she spun me around into her arms and kissed me. Suppose you could call it a kiss. It was more like a possession. Like she was trying to tattoo herself on my lips and join our souls in one kiss. Her tongue was everywhere in my mouth, her hands all over my body, and I craved more.

"Go upstairs and get naked," she whispered against my lips. The words caused a shiver of anticipation to crawl down my spine.

"But the…" I couldn't get the words out as she turned me and slapped my ass.

"I'll start the fire and get little Pounce comfortable. You, go upstairs and wait for me." I didn't even know what I was trying to argue about. I knew what she wanted, and I knew why she wanted it. As awful as she was at cutting wood, it was still attractive seeing her swing that ax. If she felt half of what I felt at seeing that, I was not surprised or shocked at her reaction. But I was the queen of sweating, and any physical activity caused me to sweat something fierce. I've always been self-conscious of it and there was no way I was lying on clean sheets sweaty.

"I need 10 minutes," I said before sprinting upstairs. I turned the shower on and jumped in to wash my body as thoroughly and as quickly as I could without making myself sweat even more.

I shivered as I stepped out of the shower and dried off. I didn't know if it was from excitement or the chill, but I didn't care to decide. I grinned as I dug through my underwear drawer. I'm sure Gianna expected me to be completely naked and as easily accessible as possible, but why not give her a little barrier to overcome? I grabbed a pair of lace panties that she could rip off of me if she really wanted to. I flushed at the thought and put them on before crawling onto the bed.

I laid on my stomach before switching to my back and putting my knees up. But that seemed silly, so I rolled onto my side with my head propped on my head staring at the stairs. That felt silly as well, so I went back on my back with my one leg bent and one leg straight, but that felt weird, too. How could one be sexy?

I laid back on my stomach and bent my legs, so my feet were in the air. Gianna loved my ass so why not make it the first thing she saw? I dropped my elbow to the bed and propped my head on my hand, but it felt unnatural. I put my head flat on the bed, but realized I looked like an idiot with nothing up but my feet. I grabbed a pillow and put it under my head wrapping my arms around it.

That felt even more stupid.

The sound of footsteps on the stairs made me quickly chuck the pillow aside and put my elbow on the bed and rested my head on my hand. I tried to look as nonchalant as possible when her head appeared.

It was unfair how fucking beautiful this woman was. Fully clothed and her hair covered with a knit hat, she was still striking. Her eyes seemed to glow with their respective colors as she took me in. My skin heated as her gaze trailed from my face down the slope of my back, up the curve of my ass, her eyes narrowed as she caught sight of the white lace. But she perused all the way to the tips of my toes before looking back to my face.

"Hi," I whispered, breaking the silence that spread across the room like a fog. It wasn't awkward, but it was so heated that if I didn't break it, I feared I might combust.

"Hi." The want in Gianna's voice made my skin erupt in goosebumps. She hadn't even touched me yet, but I could already feel the wetness between my legs. "What are those?" she asked, nodding to the lace that covered me from her.

I opened my mouth to respond, but she started to slowly take off her shirt. My mouth dried when I saw she wasn't wearing a bra. Her breasts were completely exposed to the cool air and all I wanted to do was take her nipple in my mouth.

"I thought I said to get naked?" she continued, dropping her hands to her jeans, the edge of her boxers peeking over the top of them. She slowly undid her pants and the sound of her zipper lowering intensified the heat in my lower belly.

"You did," I finally answered.

"So why are you wearing underwear?"

A boldness hit me and maybe it was from the desire that showed in her eyes and movement, but I knew what I wanted. "I thought you might like to rip them off of me."

Gianna chuckled. "Is that a me thing, or something you want?"

My breath hitched as her boxers hit the ground and she stood before me gloriously naked. Her body wasn't curvy, she had always been built straight. But she was angular and soft and full. The softness of her stomach, thighs that just brushed together, perfect breasts, and a sharp collarbone. I had never noticed collarbones before, but with Gianna, I noticed everything. And her collarbones were beautiful.

"I want it," I finally said.

"Hmm." She slowly approached the bed leaning over to run her fingers across my ass. "Do you know what I want?"

I shook my head and mourned the loss of touch when she stood and walked over to the bedside table. My brow furrowed in confusion as she turned towards me with a smile, but I realized a second too late what she was going to do.

She yanked open the drawer and made a noise of interest as she peered inside of it.

"What..." I didn't finish the question as she pulled out my favorite toys. I stared at her as she inspected it, a wicked smile curved her lips.

Gianna twisted it around in her fingers, caressing the clit stimulator and suction. "I want to play."

Chapter Twenty-Four
Gianna

"Play?" Raven's voice quivered as I turned the toy on the powerful vibration tingled up my arm. I turned it off before looking at her. Her face was bright, her cheeks flushed, and her eyes wide with excitement. Her tongue peaked between her lips and the trail of moisture was almost my undoing.

"Yes." I knelt on the bed, grabbed either side of Raven's underwear and pulled. The resulting rip and squeak from Raven sent a bolt of pleasure through me.

"Did you just–"

I held up the frayed fabric.

"Oh."

"Yes, *oh*. Now roll over."

She didn't hesitate, her eyes bounced between the toy still in my hand and my eyes.

I kissed her before moving to the edge of the bed. I noticed how quickly her chest rose and fell, how her breath panted out, and how she tried to control her squirming. When I reached her feet, I dropped to my knees, grabbed her legs, and tugged her down until her ass was at the edge of the bed. I draped her legs over my shoulders and stared down at her.

"Gianna," she said.

I looked up to see her propped on her elbows staring at me. Instead of answering, I leaned forward and ran my tongue up the seam of her pussy. Her eyes rolled and she let out a long groan that matched mine. I would never get enough of the taste of her. Never get enough of seeing her come undone because of me.

"Let me know if it becomes too much," I say holding the tip of the toy to her clit. I watched her, waiting for her consent before moving.

"Okay," she whispered, and I turned it on. The first setting was a powerful, concentrated vibration. Her back arched as the near-silent toy pulsed against her.

"Is this what you used the first night I was here?"

"Yes," she gasped in pleasure and embarrassment.

"You're not nearly as quiet as you think you are, baby girl." I moved the toy off her clit and suctioned my mouth to it instead, feeling her body convulse.

"Gods," Raven moaned. Her legs wrapping around my shoulders pulling me closer, her hands digging into my hair as I clicked a different setting, this one thumped against her, and I took the flesh of her thigh into my mouth, sucking it hard enough to mark. I wanted her covered in me completely. I wanted everything she ever saw to remind her of me.

I knew that in the moments she spent alone, she was over-thinking what we were doing. That she was trying to convince herself that we wouldn't lose each other over this, instead we could gain everything. Raven had always been embedded in my soul since the day we met, and she helped me through the anger and sadness that nearly ate me alive. Without her, I wouldn't be here.

Raven's thighs clenched around my head, pulling me closer to her. I knew she was close by the quick thrust of her hips. I pressed my palm flat to her stomach as I held the toy in place. When she came, it was loud. I set the toy on the table beside me and put my mouth on her, biting her clit.

She groaned at the sensation when I ran my tongue along her, over and over. I moved slowly, edging away the over-stimulation and bringing out new pleasure. Before I could decide if I wanted to use a second toy or continue with my mouth, Raven's legs were off my shoulders, and I was on my back on the carpet with her lips on mine.

Raven leaned on her forearms which were braced around my head, and she straddled my waist. I wrapped my arms around her, pulling her body flush with mine. There was no feeling in the world like Raven on top of me, especially naked. She was my own personal security blanket, and I would never get enough. Raven grinned and, surprising me again, she turned around and placed her pussy right over my face. I didn't even have a chance to react before I felt her mouth on me.

An near inhumane sound came from me as her teeth grazed my clit and her tongue followed. I wrapped my hands around her hips and pulled her down to me. She fit so perfectly in my mouth that there was no doubt in my mind that she had been made for me. I wanted to savor the feel of her on me and the taste of her, but I was borderline feral. I wanted her dripping into my mouth, I wanted to ring every bit of pleasure she had left in her body.

Raven was overwhelming, the taste of her in my mouth and the feeling of being in hers at the same time. I wanted to focus on bringing her to orgasm, but she was fucking magic with those lips and tongue. She ground into my face while my hips lifted into hers. We were chasing that high together and it took one bite for her to spasm, and we crashed together.

When we finally made it back downstairs, Pounce was passed out in front of the fire and the food was cold. But I made us both a plate while Raven made coffee. We sat on the couch, cuddled beneath a blanket, and Raven's fuzzy sock-covered feet rested on mine as we ate. The heater was still broken, but the fire was pleasantly warm. Plus, it allowed me to be closer to her. Even with as much sex as we had, there was nothing like being intimate without the sex. Being in Raven's orbit was like nothing you could experience earthly.

"These are the best hash browns I have ever had," Raven said around a mouthful of food.

I snorted. "They're practically frozen."

"Still good." Raven shrugged. She leaned over and kissed my cheek. "It only took 20 years of friendship for you to learn how to season."

I gasped. "How dare you! Nan will be very upset to hear that you said she can't cook."

Raven choked. "I did not say that! You better not tell her I said that!"

"You know how Nan feels about her cooking." I took another bite of food, and grinned at Raven's glare. I waited until she took another large bite of sausage before speaking again. "It's your birthday tomorrow."

Her inhale caused her to choke and cough. Raven never liked being the center of attention, thus she never liked her birthday. However, when she discovered Paganism, she learned that her birthday fell on Winter Solstice, December 21st. The longest night of the year, the start of Yule, and the turn of winter. It didn't make her enjoy it more, but it helped her not hate it. So since she was 14 years old, she celebrated Yule, and her birthday was an afterthought.

"Did you have anything planned?" I asked.

"Just the usual." She shrugged.

"Dancing naked in the snow while burning candles and sacrificing birds?"

"I've moved on to goats."

I chuckled. "Poor Mr. Tumnus." I put my empty plate on the table and faced Raven.

"I thought I would have had time to prepare, but I didn't expect the storm to last this long. I'm going to have to make some candles today."

"Can I help?"

Raven raised a brow. "You want to help me make candles?"

I nodded.

"Do you want to celebrate with me?" she whispered.

Chapter Twenty-Five
Raven

It was my first birthday without my mom.

My first Yule.

My parents were accepting from the beginning once I became a Pagan. They never questioned my choices or made me feel like what I celebrated was any less valid than the "traditional" beliefs. My mother always accepted me in whatever I chose. When I thought I would be a singer for a few months in middle school, she signed me up for singing lessons knowing that there was not one tune I could hit.

Yule and my birthday were bittersweet this year. My mother always made a feast and set the largest bonfires. She did hours of research for my first Yule and spent days preparing for it. She bought hundreds of candles, got a dozen Yule logs to light, bought rocking chairs, and so much mistletoe I thought we would never get the smell out of the house.

But it was perfect. She brought out a serving table and we gorged on food, rocked our chairs by the fire, and stared at the stars. It was before they bought the farm, so we had it in our small backyard. Gianna and her Nan joined us almost right away. Nan had made some cupcakes and Gianna brought a gift–a tarot deck. It was my first deck, and I still have it.

This might be my first without my mom and my first with Gianna as so much more than my best friend, but not much else had changed over the years. Even when we moved to the farm and when I went to college, Gianna always found a way to celebrate with me.

When we were 17, she showed up to the cabin on a motorcycle in the snow with two dozen cookies from Nan, a beautiful necklace with the moon phases, a box of bath bombs, a giant birthday candle, and an ornament-making kit. We spent the night crafting and redecorating the tree. It was my last Yule/birthday before college, and it was perfect. My best friend, my mom, and me. My dad was there, of course, but he was not as involved in the celebration. Though he supported me, he was more of a Christmas person, which I don't fault him for. He never turned his back on me or made me feel like what I believed was any less justified than his own, but he let me find my own way of living and spirituality. It was also his idea to erase "Christmas" from Moonlight Lake Tree Farm.

The snow had picked up outside again, and the snowflakes were large and incessant. It had grown about two inches in the last 30 minutes so that erased any hope of having a fire outside. Instead, we set up the fireplace. We stacked the logs up beside it, the water in Pounce's pool had been changed, and he was swimming back and forth with a coconut on his stomach while making small sounds of delight. I couldn't even name a dog that was as happy as Pounce. He may not be in the wild, but he is just as free as any other otter in Colorado.

It might not be the normal Yule/birthday celebration, but all that mattered was celebrating. Gianna's parents had been religious but considered themselves... *progressive*. She told me how much of a culture shock it was moving in with her grandparents since they did not have one religious bone in their bodies. To them, Christmas was all about presents and spending time with family. It was also Nan's favorite day, but Gianna always made Yule special for me.

And making it special is exactly what she did. While I didn't have the elaborate display I normally did, it was everything.

Gianna sat beside me through every meditation and talked through whatever was on my mind. It was special, it was private, and it was ours.

Chapter Twenty-Six
Gianna

A few days after Raven's birthday, we were sitting in the living room as Raven lit another log. She would burn the fire with one yule log every day until the first of January.

"Let's play some poker," I said as Raven situated logs in the fireplace.

She turned and arched a brow at me, fighting her smirk by taking her bottom lip between her teeth. "Poker?" she asked.

"Yes." I nodded.

"You don't like gambling."

"I do with you... and when it's strip poker."

Raven's laugh was loud, and I didn't fight the grin in response. When people are in love, they always claim that the one they love lights up every room they walk into. Well, I can honestly say that's not Raven. She was a silent beauty, never drawing attention to herself and usually sneaking into spaces. She wasn't one for attention.

No, it was Raven's laugh that drew people to her. It was infectious in its sincerity. She wasn't one for frivolity, laughing to make someone feel better or lighten a situation. Raven sat in discomfort to allow others to shine, and it was honestly beautiful.

"Are you that insatiable that you want to sleep with me again already?" she asked, grinning.

"I just said strip poker, baby girl. I said nothing about fucking," I murmured.

Her cheeks took an adorable pink hue. Raven stood and brushed her hands together, the fire illuminating her in a soft glow. The cabin had the best lighting I had ever seen, especially at sunset. The proof was staring me in the eyes. The colors caressed the side of her face while the fire lit her back. I was captivated over this woman. She was everything, and I was so in love.

A deck of cards, a bottle of wine, and two wine glasses sat on the coffee table between us. Pounce had retired from his pool and was sprawled on the couch behind me. Raven had demanded to sit before the fireplace because "if I was going to make her strip down to her underwear, the least I could do was let her be warm in front of the fireplace."

"Do you remember…" Raven started, grabbing the deck, and shuffling. Why watching her fingers move dexterously over the playing cards was so attractive, I would never fucking know, but help me if I wasn't drooling at the sight of it. I tried to pull myself together. My goal was to not jump her bones at the end of this.

Step two, let her see what life with you could be.

It wasn't all about sex, not that the sex wasn't perfect, but I wanted more. I wanted intimacy—real intimacy that wasn't just about the physical. To have real conversations, to see every imperfection on her perfect body and mind.

I had thoroughly consumed her body, I had wormed my way into her mind, and now, I wanted her soul. If that didn't make me sound like the world's most obsessed serial killer, I don't know what would. I didn't want to wear her skin, but I wanted to wear her thighs like a scarf.

Raven stared at me. Her eyebrow raised and a slight curve pulled on the corner of her lips. "What are you daydreaming about over there?"

"Nothing," I murmured.

"You remember then?"

"Remember what?"

Raven chuckled and dealt the cards, two to each of us and three out face up before us. She tapped her cards. "Do you remember the first time we played strip poker?"

"You promised you would never bring that up." I groaned as my head dropped to my hands.

"I did no such thing."

That day would go down as the worst in my life. Raven had come to visit me at college while she was on a five-day break. She found out I had a crush on my friend's roommate and decided to help me get a date with them. They were in a few of my classes and when I found out my friend knew them, I did everything I could to put myself in their orbit. But still, they didn't notice me. I thought they were playing hard to get or pretending, but I quickly realized that they were so involved in their studies that anything else paled in comparison.

Raven thought it was hilarious when I told her about my obsession and decided to help me out. She organized a little dorm party with about 10 people, nothing big, but they were there. And they smiled at me. And I decided that strip poker was a great game to play. Somehow, we ended up combining strip poker with tequila shots, and I was the only one in my boxers and sports bra. So, before I lost the last hand, and instead of standing in the room naked, I agreed to streak down Greek Row.

"I hope you've been practicing since then." Raven laughed. "What's your wager?"

I looked at my cards: seven of hearts and four of spades.

The three cards between us showed the four of diamonds, six of clubs, and six of hearts. I glanced back up to Raven to gauge her reaction. The corner of her mouth might be raised, or it might be tilted down in a frown. There might have been a line between her brows, or it might have been the light. Raven took a sip of her wine and when her eyes met mine, there was a smile as she caught me staring.

"What's wrong, Gi," she mocked. "Don't want to streak through the end of a blizzard?"

I raised a brow. "I bet a shirt." I shrugged at her eye roll. "Not my fault you decided to forgo a bra today."

"Call," she said as she set one card aside and flipped another face up into the line. The five of spades. She raised her eyes to me expectantly, her face betraying nothing. She could have a full house right now, but a straight would beat that and she couldn't have a flush.

I tried to keep my face as straight as the one I was chasing.

"I raise you, pants," she said.

I laughed, "You want to get this over in one hand huh?"

She mocked my shrug, "Not my fault you decided to forgo boxers today."

"Sometimes the breeze is nice!" I argued, gesturing to the sweatpants. They were hers, as were all the clothes I had been wearing. "Call," I said.

Raven's smile was both radiant and terrifying. She placed one card in the discard pile and flipped one in the line.

Eight of hearts.

I sat back with a grin. "Any last words, baby girl?"

Raven took a sip of her wine and tilted her head expectantly. I flipped my cards in triumph as I lined them up with the straight, I had (miraculously) procured. It wasn't often that I won, but it felt great when it did happen.

Raven smiled around the lip of her glass and mine fell.

"You can't beat a straight," I said, my voice unsure.

Raven didn't speak, instead just flipped over her two cards. Six of spades and six of diamonds.

The smile that lit Raven's face was mockingly radiant. It was both endearing and annoying and beautiful and frustrating.

"I can't believe you…" I said, slumping back into the cushions.

"Where's my strip tease?" Raven asked, her eyes twinkling.

"I'll strip for you, Raven. But just know, that this doesn't end in sex." Raven's brow furrowed as I stood and grabbed her hands, pulling her up. I grabbed our wine glasses. "Drink." We watched each other as we drank the rest of our wine, her eyes over the glass glittered with intensity. I knew what she wanted, but I didn't want this to just be about sex. I grabbed the bottle of wine and topped off our glasses. "Let's go to bed."

She opened her mouth to argue, but I kissed her and tugged her hand. She followed without complaint, her fingers gripped mine tight, as if she thought something significant was going to happen. Pounce followed us up the stairs and curled onto his little hammock and fell asleep instantly.

I grabbed Raven's glass and put it on the bedside table before turning to face her. Raven's brown eyes were bright in the dim room, the string lights she had around the space were the only light. I took her face in my hands and brushed a kiss across her mouth before taking a step back. She watched, paralyzed as I grabbed the hem of my shirt and lifted it over my head. The sound of her gulp and my shirt dropping was loud in the silent room. My sweatpants were next and she watched as I tucked my thumb into the waist band and dragged them down my legs. Raven's eyes heated my exposed skin and I tingled everywhere.

I reached back to unclasp the last barrier I had from her hungry gaze, and when it dropped, I felt the flush rise on my chest and up to my face. Even though this woman had seen me naked dozens of times this felt... fervent. Raven took in every part of my body, each scar, divet, and mole.

"You're so fucking beautiful," she whispered. I thought my heart was going to flutter out of my chest at her words. "My turn."

"You don't..." I didn't get the words out before her shirt was on the floor. She wasn't wearing a bra and my eyes immediately went to the little beauty mark that sat just above her right breast. Next came her shorts and her underwear, until she was just as naked as I was.

I had seen her naked, taken in the curves of her body, fucked her senseless, but this was the most intimate we had ever been. I wanted her.

I was fucking burning for her. The primal side of me wanted to bend her over the bed and have her cumming all over my hand.

She reached for my waist, but I intercepted her hand and threaded our fingers.

"We aren't going to have sex tonight, Raven." A flash of hurt crossed her eyes and I pulled her closer, careful to keep our bodies far enough to not touch. "Intimacy is more than orgasms and I want to make sure you know this is so much more than sex to me.

There was another side that won though. I took her hand and pulled back the blankets, she crawled into them and I followed. The fabric was cool on my heated skin and I melted into it, keeping close to Raven but not touching her.

She laid on her side and curled her hands under her pillow her eyes on mine.

"Did you know." I said, "that you have three different browns in your eyes?"

She shook her head, "I didn't know that."

"Whenever the light hits your eyes just right, it's like a colorwheel." That's exactly what the light was doing too. Hitting her eyes in a way that made all the brown speckles within stand out.

"Did you know that your eyes are different colors?" Raven asked.

"I had no idea," I laughed.

"The blue right here,"–her hand hovered over my left eye that was mostly brown, "it's my favorite." She didn't touch me as she lowered her hand again. "Where did you get the scar on your hip?"

I blinked in surprise. I guess she really had taken in everything when she watched me undress. "I ran into the corner of Nan's table when she stole my phone and was going to profess my undying love for you through text," I answered. Raven's laugh was a balm on my soul even as her eyes nearly bulged out of her head at my mention of love.

"Nan is a 15 year old in a 80 year old body," Raven chuckled.

"What about the indent on your thigh?" It looked like a chunk had been taken out of her flesh. It wasn't big, but it was big enough for me to feel when I had her legs wrapped around my head. My core throbbed at the thought.

Raven snorted. "I was stuck between a mountain lion and a hard place…"

Chapter Twenty-Seven

Raven

I would never tire of sleeping in Gianna's arms. She was sprawled across half my body. Her head rested on my chest and her breath fanned across my nipple. One of her arms was draped across my waist and a leg was sandwiched between mine.

Even though her hair was short and the sides shaved, it was still wild from her sleep. Out of the many things I adored and admired about Gianna, her ability to sleep like the dead was at the top. She was my weighted blanket, and I never wanted the feeling to end. I ran my fingers through her short, tangled locks–the red a beautiful contrast to my dark skin.

I loved Gianna. There was no doubt about that. I knew in sixth grade when she convinced every kid in our class to destroy their science projects because a basketball knocked mine over when I was walking into school and got ruined. The teacher was forced to give us another week because she couldn't give zeros to 16 students.

We all got together during the weekend and helped each other build new ones. I still don't know how she convinced them to do it, but we all got A's from that assignment which was a nice change for the teacher who normally never gave higher than a B. It wasn't the first time Gianna had done something so extreme for me, but it was the one that made the butterflies in my stomach nearly combust.

I had delved so deep into this whirlwind of being snowed in with her that I hadn't even considered what would happen after. The knowledge that if this ended badly and I lost her was terrifying. My fingers shook in her hair at the thought of it. While I couldn't bring myself to regret what had happened between us, I was scared of ruining it.

Ruining us.

Jasmin ended it with me because she claimed I was "too much" and simultaneously, "not enough", even though she was the one who cheated and made my life hell for the rest of college. I felt the vein in my neck pound and my hands turned clammy. It was hard enough losing someone I *thought* was my best friend, but the possibility of losing Gianna, who I *knew* was my person, was incomprehensible.

As if she could sense the direction of my thoughts, her arm tightened around my waist, wrapping around my back and pressing me into her.

I tried to calm my heart and staunch the panic that roared in my ears, but I could only see Gianna turning her back on me, disappearing from my life and leaving me completely alone. A vice strangled my heart, and I tightened my grip on Gianna as I blinked the burning in my eyes back.

Gianna sat up and leaned over, her body suspended over mine. She stared down at me, her eyes full of worry. Mingled with that worry was a softness that calmed the fear in my heart.

"You've been stressing, baby girl," she whispered, running a finger down the space between my brows where I knew lines sat prominently. Gianna leaned down placing her naked chest to mine and bracing her weight on her forearms. "What's going on in that beautiful head?"

I didn't want to tell her. I didn't want her to think I was comparing her to Jasmin. I wasn't. But the irrational fear still lingered.

"Nothing," I lied.

Gianna clicked her tongue and kissed my forehead, the space between my brows, and my nose before reaching my lips. "You know," she said as she ran her nose up the side of my neck. "The vein right here always tells me when you're lying." She placed a kiss on said vein. "You can tell me anything, Raven." Gianna's earnest eyes met mine.

I always knew I could tell her anything, I had always been able to, and that only hurt more. "I'm scared." The confession sat heavily on my heart.

"Of us?"

I could only nod, my throat dry and chest tight. Gianna sighed and rested her forehead on mine. My heart pounded so hard in my chest that I thought it might bust through its protective cage.

Gianna didn't respond with words. Instead, she pressed her soft lips against mine, her body rested fully on me, and I welcomed the weight of her. She felt like home, her weight an embrace I craved every time she left. Her hands roamed down my sides, pushing the sheet off of us as she kissed me, her leg raised between mine to press into the center of me. A moan came unbidden from the back of my throat. Gianna's fingers dug into my hips as if she wanted to mark me.

I reveled in the feeling of being tethered to her, of being claimed by her. I touched her everywhere I could reach, my fingers gliding on her skin that was as soft as silk. Gianna's lips left mine as she kissed down my cheek to my ear.

"You will never lose me," she whispered taking my earlobe into her mouth. She kissed down my jawline to my chin. "You could tell me right now that you want to stay friends and I will continue to be the best friend you have ever had." Gianna's mouth met mine, but she didn't kiss me, it was the softest pressure against my lips as she whispered. "You could tell me that you want to marry me, and I would slide a ring"–she caressed my ring finger, –"on this beautiful finger."

I was lightheaded with her words; last night she refused to touch me, claiming that intimacy was more than orgasms and she was right. But this feeling was more than intimacy, this was everything I had read about in books and seen in movies. This was the feeling of two souls merging to be... more.

"Take all the time you need, Raven, I'm not going anywhere." She brushed a curl from my face and wrapped a hand around my jaw. "I told you before that you decide where this goes. If you don't want this to progress past these few days, okay. But I know what I want, baby girl. I want you, and I will be here when you're ready to admit that you want me, too."

Gianna kissed me before moving her lips down to my neck. "We can take this as slow as you want." She licked the disloyal vein at my throat. "We don't have to make any decisions right now." She trailed down to my chest, taking my nipple between her teeth. Her hands pushed my legs apart and she settled between them. Her mouth and tongue left a trail down my chest and stomach until her tongue was inches from where I wanted it. Desire and love coursed fire through my veins as words threatened to spill past my lips. "Let's just enjoy each other."

Chapter Twenty-Eight
Gianna

I looked back at Raven who was sprawled across the bed on her stomach, the sheet just covered the lift of her ass, and her skin shined in the sunlight. I glanced at the note on my pillow before giving Pounce a quick pet and kissing his snout.

"Don't eat that, but make sure she gets it," I murmured to the otter before moving around the bed to place a kiss on the side of Raven's head. The soft snore she let out made me smile.

The snowstorm finally stopped, the roads were plowed, and I had to get to my Nan's. It was December 24th, and Nan had *another* annual party that I could not miss. The Christmas Eve party was a tradition before I lived with my grandparents, before I was even born.

Colorado weather never ceased to amaze me. After ten days of blizzard conditions, the sun was shining, and the snow melted so quickly that there were small ponds all over the place. It was nice to see that my beautiful truck was clear of the 25 inches that must have fallen over the past week and a half.

I sat in my truck and took a deep breath, reliving all that had happened in the past few days. At first, I didn't think that Raven and I would make it out as anything except best friends, but there was finally a chance for more. As soon as Raven saw that what we had was nothing to be afraid of. Her tendency to overthink could ruin a potentially once in a lifetime love, but I would never blame her for it. I fell in love with the knowledge of her chronic overthinking. I loved her because of it, not in spite.

My truck was grumpy when I started it, but she was more than happy to be moving again. The road was relatively clear with trucks still clearing the sludge.

My mind was occupied with Raven as I drove. How she looked naked in the sunshine and in the moonlight, how it felt when she was against me and her laugh vibrated through her entire body. Her face showed every emotion, it lit up when she was excited, but when she was sad, every piece of her body showed it.

The drive home went by quickly, before I knew it, I was parked in front of my apartment complex, staring up at my balcony. I loved my apartment, but my soul craved the cabin and the two creatures inside of it.

Three hours later, I knocked on Nan's door. Or tried to, there was an obnoxiously large wreath that blocked almost every part of the door aside from the bottom quarter. It was hideous. I think it was supposed to be Santa, but it looked more like a goblin. There was already music blaring from inside and the incessant stomping told me they were dancing. Although with how old they were, it usually looked like they kept freezing every few moves with their pauses.

I checked my phone to see no messages from Raven. Not that I expected any. I told her in the note to take her space and to message me when she was ready. Nan whipped the door open with, of course, a rocks glass in her hand full of amber liquid and a large piece of ice in it. The first thing I noticed was the reindeer antlers atop her head and then the pretty red dress she was wearing.

"There she is!" Nan yelled, yanking me into the apartment. She stuck her head out the door and looked around. "Where's Raven?"

I took the glass from her hand, sipped, and gagged. It was just straight fucking brandy. *Who drinks brandy anymore?*

"That's disgusting," I said, scrubbing my mouth with my hand.

Nan took the glass back and took a large gulp of her drink with a shrug. "You kids just don't have taste. Now where is my granddaughter?"

"I'm right here, Nan," I muttered, looking around the crowded house. They better have 911 on speed dial because the way some of those ladies are throwing their ass in a circle, someone is bound to break a hip or give someone a heart attack.

I put the gifts I brought under the tree and navigated around the bodies to the kitchen. I would absolutely need a drink to make it through this. Especially since Nan was right on my heels.

"Did you tell her you love her?" she asked.

"Nan–"

"Did you kiss her?"

I sighed and opened a beer, tipping the contents into my mouth.

"Or did you bang her lights out?"

I swallowed too hard, and the liquid went somewhere it wasn't supposed to and I coughed while spewing beer on the fridge. Nan didn't bother helping, she just laughed.

"That's a yes!" she said triumphantly. "Or maybe it wasn't good since she's not here. What's going on G?"

I wiped my eyes, careful of the mascara and eyeliner that I decided was a good idea to wear. I should have known better to show up here with makeup, let alone show up at all.

"Please, Nan." I coughed. "I kissed her, but you're not getting anything else out of me because it's inappropriate and makes me wildly uncomfortable. I can tell you she's at home and everything went well."

Nan put her hands up, "Sorry, sorry. I didn't mean to make you uncomfortable. Why is she at home if things went so well?"

"You know, Raven. She needs time and space."

"She better not take long; you've already waited two decades." Nan harrumphed.

"I tried to tell her to let me put up her wallpaper, but you know how stubborn Margie is." Tom said. He had been talking to me for over an hour and all I wanted to do was bang my head on the non-wallpapered wall. I went to have another drink of my beer only to discover it was empty.

"Sorry, Tom," I interrupted. "I need to use the restroom and grab another drink." I didn't wait for his response before I practically ran to Nan's room. Anything for a moment's peace. Her bed was full of jackets from the guests, but the bathroom was blessedly empty. I was assaulted by the pink that littered the space, but I closed the door and locked it behind me anyway.

I missed Raven. I missed the feeling of her hand in mine, hearing her voice, seeing her smile, and kissing her. I missed everything. I grabbed my phone from my pocket, it was eight p.m., but the only text I had was from Danny saying Merry Christmas.

I opened my text thread with Raven and my thumbs hovered over the keyboard. What would I even say? What could I say?

"Sorry I left you this morning, but I wanted you to take the time you needed without feeling pressured to tell me you love me even though I haven't said it. So please take your time, but can you text me please because I'm excessively needy and want to be in your orbit?"

I rolled my eyes at myself.

Give it a break, Gianna.

I knew exactly how Raven was, and if I didn't give her time, I would only push her away. I tapped water on my face, pulled on my green bowtie, and straightened my black shirt.

The living room seemed even more stuffy when I made my way back out. I went straight to the kitchen and grabbed another beer from the refrigerator. I opened it and brought it to my lips before turning to see Raven standing on the other side of the island.

I lowered my hand and blinked at her. I had to be imagining this, she couldn't be here. She wouldn't be. It hadn't even been a full day. But she was there, and she was breathtaking.

Raven's face was made up and her eyes highlighted with eyeliner, her lips a perfect nude. She had styled her curls in a way that looked as if she had spent hours on each coil. She was wearing a dress that matched my bowtie perfectly. A beautiful emerald green with a fitted bodice.

She was a goddess.

"What are you doing here?" I asked, dumbly. I put the beer down and walked around the island until I stood before her. She was wearing a pair of black and silver heels. I met her eye with a raised brow.

"You look amazing," she whispered.

I grinned at her and brushed my thumb across her cheek. "Look who's talking." Her smile nearly made me lose my mind. She was absolutely radiant, and she was here.

"I got your note."

I grimaced and ran a hand threw my hair, forgetting the copious amounts of mousse and gel I put in it earlier. "I didn't want to pressure you, but I didn't want you to think I was ditching you."

Raven grabbed my hand and threaded our fingers together. I stepped closer to her as she kissed my ring finger and rested her head on our hands.

"I know," she said meeting my gaze. I could see the fear and hesitation there, but also a determination that sent my already quick pulse skyrocketing. She leaned up and pressed a soft kiss to my lips. "Do you want to know what I realized when I woke up this morning and you were gone?"

"I'm sorry."

"You have nothing to be sorry for. It made me realize that while I am so scared of losing you, I'm even more afraid of not trying. I'm afraid of not being with you, Gianna. I'm so tired of letting my past dictate my future. I have always been yours, Gianna. I have been in love with you for as long as I can remember, and I don't know how not to be. I love you, Gianna. I love you so fucking much."

Her words were broken with tears, and I knew that we probably looked insane, crying in the dining room, our hands clasped. But I wanted to forever remember this moment. I had been hers since I was nine years old, I was just waiting for her to catch up. And she finally had.

I wrapped my hand around her face and pulled her lips to mine. They were as soft as they had always been, her arms went around my neck and her body pressed against mine. Nothing about the kiss was clean, it was full of tears and sniffles and held-back sobs, but it was perfect.

"I love you, Raven. I've always loved you," I said against her lips. She cried even harder as I lifted her off the ground. My heart was so full that I thought it might implode.

A roaring reached my ears and I finally noticed that not only were there other people in the room, but they were cheering for us.

"I did that! I did that!" Nan's yell was the loudest, of course. I laughed and set Raven down, my lips still pressed against hers.

"Is that your phone vibrating, or are you just happy to see me?" I slurred against her mouth. I was drunk on her and could hardly form coherent words.

Chapter Twenty-Nine

Raven

"Dad?" I asked into the phone, tentatively. My previously thrilled heart was terrified of the voice on the other line. I hadn't talked to him since I told him I wanted to buy the farm. He called for my birthday and Yule, but otherwise, he had been silent.

"Hey, kid." I smiled at the sound of his voice, apprehension fading away. He sounded happy, he sounded–were those waves?

"Dad, where are you?" I asked.

"I'm in Bermuda." Gianna watched me concerned as my mouth dropped open.

"Wha..."

"Moonlight Lake Tree Farm is in your name, kid. It's all yours."

"But–"

"I don't need the money, and you were right. Mom would have wanted you to have it and keep it running. Not for her, but for you. You've never settled anywhere for long, and the farm has always been a home for you. There must be a reason you keep coming back, right?" He laughed.

"Are you alright?" Gianna's voice was soft as her hand wrapped around my waist bringing my side flush with hers. I gaped at her, shock mixed with a coil of fear making its way down my spine. I know I had talked about keeping the farm, but now that it was mine, I was fucking petrified.

"Is that Gi? Put her on."

Wordlessly, I handed the phone to Gianna whose brow was still furrowed in concern as she put it to her ear.

"Rufus, I think you broke your daughter." I watched as Gianna's pinched brow loosened and a smile that could light up the bottom of Bryce Canyon National Park broke across her face. "Oh, you definitely broke her," she said with a laugh.

I got more irritated the longer she stayed on the phone, but her arm never loosened from my waist. When I tried to adjust, she just gripped me tighter and pulled so the front of our bodies were pressed together. Her eyes met mine as she talked, and my cheeks were so warm at the unspoken words in her eyes, I thought they might combust.

Her fingers massaged my hip through the thin fabric of my dress it was very distracting. I looked away from the heat of Gianna's eyes only to meet Nan, who had a shit-eating grin that made my eye roll compulsively. She had allowed me to have my big, I love you moment, and I knew that she was just waiting for us to give her some unintentional signal and she would make her way to us like a slingshot. She held a champagne bottle and was rocking back and forth as if preparing to bulldoze us.

"You know I will." Gianna's words pulled my eyes back to her, and I saw a soft smile on her beautiful mouth. Her hand left my waist, and she brushed her fingers across my lips. I smiled at the action. She tilted the phone away from her mouth and kissed my cheek. I could hear the muffled voice of my dad as she did, and he was moving a mile a minute. "Okay, I love you, too. Here she is."

Gianna handed the phone to me and pulled me against her again, one hand around my waist and the other at my face. I had never felt as cherished as I did in that moment as I put the phone to my ear again.

"Dad?"

"It's about fucking time," he yelled. "Your mother and I were just waiting for the day that you two would pull your heads out of your asses."

"Yes, thank you," I grumbled back.

"I'm so happy you're happy, Rav."

"I am, and I hope you are, too."

"I'm getting there. I just miss your mom so much."

My heart pulled, and as if she knew the direction of the conversation, Gianna's grip tightened on me. "I miss her too," I whispered. "Please stay safe out there."

He scoffed, "Have a great party."

"Merry Christmas, Dad."

"Happy Yule, kid."

I hung up the phone and kissed Gianna.

"Don't tell Nan she was right," Gianna murmured against my lips just as the lady in question made her way over to us.

My mouth curved into a grin as I kissed her again. "We would never hear the end of it."

"I'll have to make Danny the best man."

Epilogue
Raven

Five Years Later

"We need water," I said and stretched in the warm arms that surrounded me.

Gianna snorted, burying her face further into my neck and tightening her hold on me. "I need a full body massage is more like it." She sat up on her elbow and rubbed her tongue across her bottom lip. "Maybe a tongue massage too."

I laughed sliding from beneath her. The morning light was warm on my naked skin as I stretched before her. She plopped her head on her hand watching me with a feline interest.

"How about you grab some ice cubes and lay back down?" Gianna asked, her brow raised and the corner of her bottom lip between her teeth.

"Don't you need water? Aren't you dehydrated?"

"Tapping out on me already Mrs. McCarthy?"

I grinned at her and glanced down at the ring on her finger. The black band etched with silver was nestled on her hand like it had been made for it. Which let's face it, it had been. I would have welded that ring to her finger if I could.

I couldn't believe that I married Gianna. Actually, yes, I could. I think there was always a part of me that knew I would marry her, that we were more than just best friends.

She was my soulmate.

On my birthday, the year after we were snowed in together, she asked me to marry her. Two years later we were married in a small ceremony.

That's a lie. Nothing about our wedding was small. Especially since Nima, who swore up and down that they were low maintenance, planned it. I told them I wanted no more than 15 people which quickly turned into 75.

Still, it was a stunning ceremony, and Gianna and I were drunk for two days after. It did not stop her from ravishing me on our wedding night though. We were drunk and satiated, and I was so happy.

Over the last few years, the tree farm flourished. Gianna and I came up with plans for both of our businesses, teaming up well enough that Gianna was able to open a second, smaller mechanic shop right next to the tree farm. As much as I tried to tell her that I could give primary management to Cheryl and move with her to Caswell, she wouldn't hear it. Deserea was now part owner of the original McCarthy's and Gianna opened Moonlight Lake Mechanics. It was the stupidest name for a mechanic shop, and I told her as much, but that first opening weekend showed me that I had no idea what I was talking about. Ever.

Not everything had been great though. Nan passed right after our wedding when we got back from our honeymoon. That was a devastating blow, and it took Gianna months to recover. Funnily enough, it was Tom, Nan's *"bone buddy"* (that's what Nan had called him) who pulled Gianna out of her slump. He drove to the farm, stomped up to the cabin, and yelled at her about how Nan didn't raise her to mope and if she knew how Gianna had been acting, she would have taken her over her knee and whooped the sadness out of her. There were many more words exchanged, and Tom came downstairs taking a cup of tea from me gratefully. Pounce and I sighed with relief when we heard the shower turn on.

It still took a long time for her to find her stride without Nan, but she had gotten so much better. Dad had started dipping his toe in the dating pool. Four years of being single and traveling the world only made him feel so fulfilled, and as sad as it was to think about, he deserved happiness.

I walked to the small kitchen in the room we were staying in. We were celebrating our second wedding anniversary in Scotland. We took this trip for Nan, visiting some of her favorite places in the Highlands. It was surreal to see what I had only seen in photos she shared from her childhood.

Some of the views we saw looked almost too real. As if they were computer generated. Of course, we hit many of the tourist spots, but we also had a list of destinations from Nan. My least favorite part of the first three days was the driving. Which was why I made Gianna do the majority of it.

We spent two days in Edinburgh before we made our way over to a little flat that sat over a bakery in Inverness. It was one of the more popular destinations in the Highlands, but we were making our way over to Isle of Arran next.

I poured two glasses of water and looked out the little window over the sink. The street was starting to get busy, and the smell of freshly baked bread made its way up the floors. I walked back to where Gianna was sprawled on a makeshift pad in the living room. The bed was a little too soft for Gianna's back, so we made our own on the hardwood floor. I guzzled my water as I made my way back to her and a little splashed down my chest.

"Come here." I blinked at Gianna's raspy voice. She was staring at me, her eyes like liquid heat on my body.

I held up the glass. "Thirsty?"

"Not for water," she murmured laying on her back and biting her lip. I wish I could roll my eyes at her antics, but my bodies reaction to the desire in her voice eliminated any teasing. Even after five years, I couldn't get enough of her.

"How about," I said, slowly making my way back to where she lay, "you drink a little water first."

"Make me," she said, her smirk a roguish challenge.

I straddled her waist with my feet. Her eyes were wide as she looked to where I knew she would. I slowly dropped to my knees and sat on her stomach, careful to keep a majority of my weight on my legs. I sat my glass down and took a mouthful of her water. Gianna's hands were on my thighs her fingers trailing up and down them.

I leaned down so my mouth was hovering over hers and raised my eyebrow in a challenge. Gianna's eyes flashed and with that same sly smile she opened her mouth. Slowly, I allowed water to pass from my mouth to hers. Gianna didn't close her eyes the entire time, her mis-matched gaze locked onto mine as I quenched a little bit of her thirst.

I swallowed. "Want more?"

She shook her head and wrapped her arms around my legs and hauled my pussy up to her face.

"Happy anniversary, baby girl," she murmured before burying her face between my thighs.

Acknowledgements

Let's start this off by talking about how much of a change of pace this book was for me to write. A world without magic was difficult to create, but I adore everything about this story. I started writing Love on Moonlight Lake (affectionately called LoML) in December of 2023 when I was trying to find lighthearted sapphic romances. When Raven and Gianna presented themselves to me as a park ranger turned tree farm owner and mechanic, respectfully, I was confused as to how the hell they even met to fall in love. However, once their story started it was hard not to adore their story. LoML is the first contemporary romance I have ever written, and I have to say that I am so proud of it.

My first gratification has to go to my cover designer, Bre. She was one of the first people I told about wanting to do LoML and she not only asked to design the cover before the book was even finished, but she also helped me name it. I am forever thankful for you and your amazing talent, and I can't wait to see how far you go in this industry. You deserve the world.

To my editors, Al and Ash. You two are phenomenal. I'm writing this after your edits so any errors you find... let's give me a little pass on that, okay? I can't thank you enough for being as amazing as you are and putting in the time and effort that you do. I am grateful to D.W. Cole for leading me to you. I would be remiss to not take this opportunity to give D.W. Cole's Rotten Fruit a shout-out. A beautifully tragic story by the most kindhearted soul ever.

To the best beta readers a little author could ask for. Thank you for reading my trashily-edited draft and giving me such wonderful feedback. You helped me tune up the story and capture exactly what I wanted and needed for the story to be the best it could. The world doesn't deserve kindhearted souls like yours, but I'm so thankful that you're here!

Finally, to my readers. Thank you for giving me a chance. It was a one in a million possibility that you crossed my book and I am so honored that you gave LoML and me a chance. Whether you liked it or not, thank you so much for being here. If you did like it, I would say go check out my other work if you're interested. I have a fantasy series out that is my life's work.

Thank you all for giving this small indie author a chance. I am a queer author, and I write queer stories. Here's to many more stories being told by us, for us.

About the Author

Long time writer and full-time bourbon connoisseur Adriana creates character driven, emotion inducing, novels that are guaranteed to transport you to another world. Her characters, while clever and cunning, will enthrall you with raw reactions, desperate decisions, and foolish fearlessness.

In her spare time, you can find Adriana curled up with a good book, practicing tarot, or judging wine while binge watching Supernatural. Follow Adriana to keep up with new releases, book conventions or sign up for her newsletter to see what other antics she's up to.

TikTok: adrianasargentauthor
Instagram: adrianasargentauthor
Website: authoradrianasargent.com